STORY OF A GIRL

STORY OF
A GIRL

A NOVEL BY SARA ZARR

 LITTLE, BROWN AND COMPANY
New York ᴠ Boston

Little, Brown and Company

Hachette Book Group USA
237 Park Avenue, New York, NY 10017
Visit our Web site at www.lb-teens.com

First Edition: January 2007

The characters and events portrayed in this book are fictitious. Any similarity to real persons, living or dead, is coincidental and not intended by the author.

"First Lesson" from *Lifelines* by Philip Booth, copyright © 1999 by Philip Booth. Used by permission of Viking Penguin, a division of Penguin Group (USA) Inc.

ISBN 978-0-316-01453-3

10 9 8 7 6 5

Q-FF

Printed in the United States of America

For everyone who is my family.

First Lesson

Lie back, daughter, let your head
be tipped back in the cup of my hand.
Gently, and I will hold you. Spread
your arms wide, lie out on the stream
and look high at the gulls. A dead-
man's float is face down. You will dive
and swim soon enough where this tidewater
ebbs to the sea. Daughter, believe
me, when you tire on the long thrash
to your island, lie up, and survive.
As you float now, where I held you
and let go, remember when fear
cramps your heart what I told you:
lie gently and wide to the light-year
stars, lie back, and the sea will hold you.

— Philip Booth

STORY OF A GIRL

I was thirteen when my dad caught me with Tommy Webber in the back of Tommy's Buick, parked next to the old Chart House down in Montara at eleven o'clock on a Tuesday night. Tommy was seventeen and the supposed friend of my brother, Darren.

I didn't love him.

I'm not sure I even liked him.

The car was cold and Tommy was stoned and we'd been there doing pretty much the same thing a dozen times before, and I could smell the salt air from the beach, and in my head I wrote the story of a girl who surfed the cold green ocean, when one day she started paddling in the wrong direction and didn't know it until she looked back and couldn't see the shore.

In my head I wrote the story, while Tommy did his thing, one hand wrapped around my ponytail.

It was the girl — the surfer girl — I had on my mind when Tommy swore and got off of me. My dad dragged him out of the car, then me. He threw Tommy to the ground and pushed me into our old Tercel.

Right before we pulled out of the lot, I stole a look at my dad. There might have been tears slipping down his cheek, or it might have been a trick of the headlights bouncing off the night fog.

I started to say something. I don't remember what.

"Don't," he said.

That was almost three years ago.

My dad hasn't looked me in the eye or talked to me, really talked to me, since.

1.

They made us clean out our lockers on the last day of sophomore year. I tore down the class schedule I'd taped to the inside of the door at the beginning of the semester and tossed it
into the pile of recycling that already included ninety-five percent of the crap I'd busted my ass to do all year. What was the
point of all that so-called learning if, in the end, it was going
into the trash? The only stuff I kept was from Honors English.
I would deny this if asked, but I thought I might want to read
some of my essays again. There's this one from when we read
Lord of the Flies. I really got into it, the savagery and survival-
of-the-fittest stuff. A lot of kids in my class didn't get it. Jeremy Walker asked, "Why couldn't the boys on the island just
get along?"

Then Caitlin Spinelli was all, "Yeah, didn't they know their chances for survival were, like, so much better if they worked together?"

Hello! Walk down the halls of your own school for three seconds, Spinelli: we *are* savages. There is no putting of the heads together to come up with a better way. There is no sharing of the bounty of popularity with those less fortunate. There is no pulling along of the deadweight so that we can all make it to the finish line. At least not for me. Caitlin Spinelli might have a different perspective, being rich in all the things that would have put her in the surviving tribe.

Anyway, Mr. North wrote on my essay in purple pen. He used red pen to correct spelling errors and messed-up grammar and stuff like that, but when he just wanted to let you know he liked something, he used purple.

Deanna, he wrote, *you clearly have much of importance to say.*

Much of importance.

"Yo, Lambert!"

Speaking of savages, Bruce Cowell and his pack of jock-wannabes, who'd been kicked off every school team because of attitude problems and/or the use of illegal substances, were right on schedule for their weekly feats of dumbassery.

Bruce leaned up against the lockers. "You look hot today, Lambert."

"Yeah." Tucker Bradford, flabby and red faced, came close and said, "I think your boobs got bigger this year."

I kept sorting through the stuff in my locker, peeling a piece of candy cane left from Christmas off one of my binders. I reminded myself it was the last day of school, and besides, those guys were seniors. If I could get through the next five minutes I would never have to see them again.

However, five minutes is a long time, and sometimes I just can't keep my mouth shut.

"Maybe," I said, pointing at Tucker's chest. "But they're still not as big as yours."

Bruce and the lackeys watching from a few feet away laughed; Tucker got redder, if that was possible. He leaned in with his nasty Gatorade breath and said, "I don't know what you're saving yourself for, Lambert."

This is the thing: Pacifica is a stupid small town with only one real high school, where everyone knows everyone else's business and the rumors never stop until some other kid is dumb enough to do something that makes a better story. But my story had the honor of holding the top spot for over two years running. I mean, a senior getting caught with his pants down on top of an eighth-grade girl, by the girl's *father* ("No way! Her *father*? I'd just kill myself!") was pretty hard to beat. That story had been told in hallways and locker rooms and parties and the back of classrooms since Tommy first came to school the morning after it happened. At which time he gave all the details to his friends, even though he knew it meant my brother, Darren, would kick his ass. (He did.) By the time I got to Terra Nova for ninth grade, the whole school already thought they knew everything there was to know about Deanna Lambert. Every time someone in school saw my face, I knew they were thinking about it. I knew this because every time I looked in the mirror, I thought about it, too.

So when Tucker breathed his stink all over me and said what he did, I knew it meant more than just a generic insult suitable for any girl. He reduced my whole life story into one nine-word attack. For that, I had to send him off in style. I started with the middle finger (you really can't go wrong with a classic). I followed it with a few choice words about his mother, and finished by implying that maybe he wasn't into girls.

Right about then I wondered if there were any teachers or otherwise responsible adults around in case Tucker and Bruce and their friends decided to take it beyond words. Probably I should have thought of that sooner.

Bruce chimed in. "Why do you front, Lambert? Why pretend you're not a skank when you know you are?" He gestured to himself and the guys around him, "*We* know you are. *You* know you are. And, um, your *Dad* knows you are, so . . ."

A voice called from down the hall: "Don't you guys have some kittens to go torture or something?"

Jason had never sounded so good.

"You don't *even* want a piece of this, punk," Tucker said, shouting over his shoulder.

Jason kept walking toward us, with his usual no-hurry

slouch, black boots scuffing along the floor like it was just too much effort to pick up his feet. My hero. My best friend.

"Didn't you, like, *graduate* yesterday?" he said to the guys. "Isn't it a little pathetic to still be hanging around here?"

Bruce grabbed Jason's jeans jacket and slammed him up against the lockers. Where in the hell were the people in charge? Had all the teachers fled for the Bahamas as soon as the last bell rang?

"Get off him," I said.

One of Tucker's friends said, "Come on, man, we don't have time for this shit. We promised Max we'd have the keg there by four."

"Yeah," said Tucker, "my brother only works at Fast Mart for like ten more minutes. After that, we're gonna get carded."

Bruce let go of Jason and gave me one last look, straight into my eyes. "See what a waste of time you are, Lambert?"

We watched them go down the hall and disappear around the corner. I kicked my pile of recycling and watched the papers fly.

"You okay?" Jason asked.

I nodded. I was always okay. "I have to drop off my French book, then sophomore year is officially over."

"About time. What now?"

"Denny's?"

"Let's go."

.   .   .

After Denny's, we went to the CD store and mocked the music on the listening stations, then Jason tagged along while I picked up job applications from all the stores and food places at Beach Front, a sad, tired strip mall that hardly anyone shopped at since the second Target opened over in Colma. We didn't talk much. I kept reliving Tucker's breath on me as he said what everyone at school probably thought.

Jason and I are okay without talking. That's how you know you really trust someone, I think; when you don't have to talk all the time to make sure they still like you or prove that you have interesting stuff to say. I could spend all day with him and not say a word. I could look at his face all day, too. His mom is Japanese and his dad, who died right after Jason was born, was white. Jay has this amazingly shiny black hair and long eyelashes, with his dad's blue eyes. (Why do guys always have eyelashes girls would kill for?) Frankly, I never understood why girls around here didn't throw themselves at him. Maybe because he's on the quiet side, and short, like his mom. Doesn't bother me, because we're almost the same height and would match up perfectly if there was ever any occasion for matching up.

He's laid-back. He's loyal. He gets it. In fact, the only thing wrong with Jason is that, at the time, he happened to be the boyfriend of my other best friend, Lee.

Unlike Jason, who's known me forever, Lee only recently achieved best-friend status by transferring in from a school in

San Francisco and being all cool. Not cool as in dressing right and knowing anything about music or whatever, but cool as in being the kind of person who doesn't try to be someone she is not.

I met her in PE when she did a belly flop off the vault during our lame gymnastics unit. Mrs. Winch kept saying, "Walk it off, Lee, then do it again." I was like, excuse me but I don't think she's breathing, and hell if *I'm* going to kill myself on that thing, too. We both got a zero for the day and a lecture from Mrs. Winch about our lack of "gumption."

I watched her around school after that. She's slightly on the dorky side, with this short hair that never does anything right and clothes that fall just on the wrong end of trying too hard. I figured the slightly-on-the-dorky-side group at school would take her in pretty quick — you know, the drama geeks and college entrance club people — but I watched her for a while and she didn't have anyone. Which meant she probably hadn't gotten connected enough to know about me yet. So I started talking to her and got a feeling, like she was different from most of the other girls who only cared about how they looked and were always talking smack about their supposed best friends.

Once we started hanging out, she told me that her real dad's a drunk and she didn't know where he was, and I told her that's okay, my dad hates me. When she asked why, I told her about Tommy. It felt good to be able to tell *my* version instead of Tommy's, the one that everyone at school knew. After I told her, I got worried she wouldn't like me anymore or she'd start acting weird around me, but she just said, "Well, everyone has stuff they wish they could change, right?"

So I guess it's my own fault Jason hooked up with her. I kept talking about Lee this and Lee that and Jay you should get to know Lee; you'd like her. He did.

I didn't care, really. Everyone knows that if you start fooling around with your friends, you can kiss what's best about your friendship good-bye. I tried to see it like I had the better end of the deal, that if Lee and Jason broke up, they probably wouldn't hang out anymore, whereas I would still get to be his friend.

Once in a while, though, something little would happen, like they'd be walking down the hall at school holding hands and I'd see them but they wouldn't see me, and first I'd think, God are they cute together! And then it felt like I was watching something superprivate, something that he had only with her. I always thought I knew him better than anyone, but once they started going out it was like Lee was some kind of insider in a way that I wasn't.

Jason and I still had our days, like the last day of school, when it was just us, and even though it sounds semidisloyal to say this, times like that I pretended Lee didn't exist.

Until he'd start talking about her.

". . . I got a text from Lee during fourth," he was saying. Our bus wound its way down Crespi Drive and into the flats, where we both lived. "They were on the beach in San Luis Obispo."

She and her family had left that morning for Santa Barbara, to pick up her brother from college. "When's she coming back?"

"Day after tomorrow. Her stepdad has to get back to work."

"Right."

The bus heaved to a halt at my stop, the stop I'd been getting off at my whole life, in front of a mold-gray house a few doors down from ours, with five cars parked on the lawn — cars that had been there since the dawn of time, at least.

"Call me tomorrow," Jason said.

"Yeah."

It was the worst part of every day, when the bus got to my stop and I had to leave Jason, him still rolling, still on his way to something, while I'd reached the daily dead end known as my house.

I stood outside the front door for my usual count of ten before walking inside. One, two . . . don't notice how the garage door doesn't hang straight . . . three, four, five . . . forget about the broken flowerpot that's been in a heap on the lawn since last summer . . . six, seven . . . it's okay, everyone leaves their Christmas lights up all year . . . eight . . . the front porch is a fine place for a collection of soggy cardboard boxes . . . nine . . . oh, forget it, just turn the knob and go in already.

Ten is everything else: the smell of mildew that never goes away, the five steps over green shag to go from the living room to the kitchen, the Pepto-pink walls of the kitchen, and, finally, my parents.

"You're home late." Dad, compact and self-contained, an island on a kitchen chair, didn't look up from his dinner when he said it. "Better get started on your homework."

"It was the last day of school, Dad."

His fork paused for a second, then he kept eating. "I know. I'm just saying that I hope you plan to stay out of trouble this summer." As if I'd been in all kinds of trouble, which I hadn't, not for a long time. "Did you hear what I said?"

"Yeah."

Mom's cheery voice chimed in the way it always does when she sees a subject that needs changing. "Why don't you sit down and have some dinner with us?"

"I ate."

"Well, then, dessert," she said, heaping more food onto Dad's plate, her dyed and fried hair falling over her face. "How about some ice cream?"

Mom's favorite phrases are:

1. *Your father just isn't very expressive.* (Interchangeable with *Just because he doesn't say he loves you doesn't mean he doesn't feel it.*)
2. *We simply need to put it behind us; be a good girl and it will be all right.*
3. *How about some ice cream?*

"Is Darren home from work yet?" I asked.

"Stacy just left for work and to drop off the car," Mom said. "Or pick up the car. I can never remember how it works."

Darren still lived at home, which wasn't exactly the plan — not for him, not for my parents. When his girlfriend, Stacy, got pregnant and decided to keep the baby, their only option was to move into our basement and give up on anything resembling a plan.

He and Stacy both worked at Safeway — Darren days and Stacy nights — so that one of them could always be with the baby, April. Which was a good system, I guess, except that they never saw each other unless they were handing off the keys to their one car.

"Stacy got out of here late, as usual," Dad said. "She's lucky they don't fire her."

"She's made employee of the month twice," I reminded him as Mom handed me a bowl of fudge brownie ice cream that I hadn't asked for.

Dad waved his napkin. "It's no excuse." He liked Stacy about as much as he liked me.

"Oh, I don't know," Mom said, "I'm sure they give her a little leeway, being a new mother and all . . ."

I set my ice cream down and left them there to discuss Stacy's career while I went in search of the one person in the house I actually *wanted* to talk to.

She was in her car seat on my parents' bed, all mellow from her afternoon nap. "Hi, April," I said, picking her up. I kissed her little face for a while and took her to my room: *my* ten-by-twelve piece of unoccupied territory, *my* piles of clothes and *my* CDs and *my* macaroni-art Thanksgiving turkey from third grade, still hanging over my bed. I spread a blanket on the carpet, laid April on her stomach, and sat next to her.

I was there when April was born. I didn't really want to be. From what I'd seen in health ed and also in movies and on *ER,* with all the screaming and pushing and blood and slime and sweat, I'd just as soon wait to see the baby after it was clean and dried and fed and, most importantly, asleep. It was Darren who wanted me in the delivery room. He said it was because Stacy was upset that her mom refused to come, and she wanted another girl there. But I knew that Darren was nervous; he didn't want to be there alone if anything went wrong.

Nothing went wrong. I didn't actually see April come out, thank God. I stood up at Stacy's head and stayed focused on her and tried to block out all the noises and smells. When Darren said, "Holy shit, she's here," I looked up and saw April in his hands, shaking all over and wailing like she was beyond pissed. It was amazing, really.

It took me a while to get used to her. All she did was cry and poop and sleep, and to be honest, she was kind of ugly. Plus there were so many rules about how to hold her and feed her; I was too stressed to enjoy it. Then she got less ugly and made more interesting sounds and wasn't so fragile. And *everything* changed when she started to recognize my voice. There was something about the way she got quiet and turned her head to me when I talked that made me feel like maybe I wasn't such a screwup after all.

When I was with Darren and Stacy and April, I could picture us going on forever. I imagined coming home from school to wherever we all lived — not at my parents' house, obviously — and April would be waking up from a nap, maybe, and Stacy would say, *Hey, Deanna, thank God you're home. I need a break and you're so good with April. . . . Would you watch her while I go get Darren from work?* And I'd say, *Sure, no problem, take your time.* And I'd play with April, maybe, like, an educational game so that she'd get smart, and Darren and Stacy would come back and we'd eat dinner and I'd do my homework while we all watched TV. I mean, I knew it wouldn't be perfect like that all the time, but it would be home.

This was my plan:

I'd get a job, right, and work my butt off all summer, then Darren and Stacy and me would pool our money and find a place. I hadn't told anyone yet; it was all about timing. I wanted to wait until I had a stack of cash saved up. I already knew exactly how I'd tell them: I'd get all my money out of the bank — in tens and twenties, so that it looked like a lot — and go down to the basement to show Darren and Stacy. I'd do it some night when Dad was really off his chain, driving us nuts, and I'd throw it on the bed without a word.

Stacy would get all hyper and Darren would just count it, looking up at me like, *Wow, that's my little sister.*

It would be obvious, then. They'd see how much easier things would be with me around.

MOST POPULAR VERSIONS OF THE STORY

"Deanna Lambert is a total nympho. Tommy would be at her house, right, hanging with Darren. As soon as Darren leaves the room, Deanna comes around and tells Tommy all this nasty stuff she wants to do with him. This one time? She told Tommy that she knew where Darren kept his porn magazines and she wanted Tommy to look at them with her. And do all this . . . *stuff.* Tommy's like, *No way, you're too young, I could get arrested,* but she begged him and begged him and finally he took her out. I heard that when her dad caught them, it took her forever to get out of the car because she was into getting tied up. What a slut!"

"Deanna Lambert is a complete psycho. Tommy liked her at first because he thought she was sweet and cute. Then they started going out and she'd be cutting herself, or all cranked on meth, or coming up with crazy ideas like they should bomb the school or whatever. When he tried to break up with her, she was like, *I'm gonna kill myself if you leave me, Tommy*! What a nightmare!"

"Deanna Lambert is beyond pathetic. Tommy first met her when he found her crying in the backyard at Darren's house. She said no one loved her, no one paid any attention to her, and pretty soon she's hanging on to Tommy like *he's* the one who's going to fix everything. Yeah, Tommy Webber. I know. Well, he felt sorry for her. He took her out for ice cream this one time when Darren wasn't home, thinking it would cheer her up, but she acted like he'd *proposed* or something. She kept calling him and calling him and finally he's like, *Okay, I'll go out with you but remember I'm seventeen and if you want to be my girlfriend, well, you gotta* do *stuff*. She said, *Anything, I'll do anything you want*. What a loser. I mean, get some self-respect."

2.

The stories in my head about the girl on the waves, the story I started that night with Tommy, didn't get onto paper until I had Mr. North for English. One time in class he said we should keep a journal, and I thought, no thanks, that whole dear diary thing is so fourth grade. Then he said a journal could be anything, like drawings or poetry or lists or whatever, anything you wanted to say about anything and no one else would ever see it. Jeremy Walker said, "Then what's the point? Are you saying we don't get credit?"

"The point," Mr. North said, sweeping a floppy piece of gray hair over his forehead, "is to have a place to express your personal feelings. You *do* have personal feelings, don't you, Jeremy?"

Everyone laughed, ha ha ha, and Mr. North hardly ever mentioned journals again, but I bought a two dollar comp book at Walgreens and started writing down these little things about the girl, just random stuff. The girl on her surfboard, the girl with her family, the girl on the beach, whatever.

One day I read what I had and thought, God but that sucks, ripped out the pages and threw them away. I mean, Mr. North said, "Express your personal feelings." He didn't say, "Write a bunch of boring crap-ass nonsense about a made-up person doing nothing."

The weird thing is, after I tore those pages up? I missed her. I missed the girl in my head. So I started in again, this time staying away from the once-upon-a-time stuff and trying to stick to "personal feelings."

Personal feelings I didn't want to feel, I gave to her.

Like if my dad spent yet another evening ignoring me and I started thinking about how I'd worshiped him when I was a kid, I might write:

The girl remembered running down the driveway toward him, cement cold under her tiny feet.

She's been waiting, always waiting, for him to come home. It is the best part of the day.

I was working on some of that stuff the next morning, when Lee called to let me know she'd gotten back from Santa Barbara.

"It's nice," she said, "but I wouldn't want to live there. Lots of tall, blond people with really white teeth. I feel like a troll whenever I visit. Oooh, look at that short person with brown hair! How did *she* get in?"

I studied the page in my comp book.

~~The girl thought of the sea, rolling and thick and dangerous.~~
The girl thought of the sea, flat and steely. Dead.

"That's one good thing about Pacifica," I said, closing the book and letting it drop to the floor. "You can be totally average and still look better than half the population."

"Save me from my family, Deanna. My mom is having a 'sing-along to Simon & Garfunkel while we clean the house' kind of morning."

I smiled into the phone at Lee's deadpan delivery. The girl cracks me up. "I'm going down to Beach Front later to drop off job applications. Wanna come with?"

"Let's meet at the donut shop," she said. "I've been donut deprived. I don't think people in Santa Barbara are allowed to eat donuts."

I got dressed and went down to the basement to see what Stacy and April were up to.

Darren had left for work before I woke up; Stacy was in bed with April, watching TV. The basement room was small and not exactly what you'd call decorated. Two windows looked out onto the sidewalk — windows that had blackout shades but no curtains — and there were a couple of cheap pieces of furniture they got at Target, and the TV. The only other things were a few snapshots of Darren and Stacy and April tacked to the wall, and of course Stacy's lighthouses. She was semiobsessed with them. On her birthday, right after she found out she was pregnant, Darren took her to this lighthouse down the coast for a picnic lunch and for, like, two weeks after that she could hardly stop smiling. She had all kinds of pictures of lighthouses that she'd torn out of magazines and printed off the Internet, and a big poster of one right over April's crib.

"How'd she sleep?" I asked.

"Excellent. She woke up only once." Stacy dug into the pile of clean laundry next to her. "Crap. I can't find her purple thing, the thing, the jumper or onesie or layette or whatever it's called."

I sorted the laundry and found the thing Stacy was looking for stuck to one of April's baby blankets. "Here. It's a onesie. I think."

Everything was kind of a mess. Stacy and my dad fought about that all the time. I guess you couldn't really call it fighting since my dad is more the quiet-angry kind of person than the yelling-angry kind, but he kept making comments about Stacy's housekeeping habits, along with her work habits and parenting habits, not to mention her clothes habits. She tended to dress, well, trashy.

I watched her as she put the onesie on April, remembering

how scared I used to be of her before she and Darren hooked up. She and Corvette Kim owned the school back then, when they were seniors and I was a freshman. Not like the *school* school, not the cafeteria or gym or halls. Those were strictly the territory of jocks and cheerleaders and wannabes. Stacy and Kim and their friends were like the Mafia, lurking around in the parking lot and the upper soccer field and the strip of Terra Nova Boulevard between the flagpole and the tennis courts. It's not like they'd *do* anything to you if you ran into them, not usually. But you didn't really even want them to *look* at you. For a long time I wanted to be Stacy, that tough and cool and grown-up. I would have killed for that kind of power at school.

Stacy the Teenage Mother handed April to me and got up. "I guess I should at least make the bed. Hey, can you watch April for a couple of hours this morning?"

"I'm meeting Lee down at Beach Front to drop off some job applications," I said. April grabbed a fistful of my hair and started pulling.

"Don't let her do that," she said, with that old edge of toughness she'd never lost. "I'm trying to teach her to stop."

"I can watch her when I get back if you want," I said, gently prying my hair out of April's tiny hand.

Stacy shook her head. "She has a checkup this afternoon."

"Oh. Sorry."

"No big deal. I just wanted to go to some thrift stores in the city to look for clothes. My old stuff still doesn't fit. I feel like such a cow."

April grabbed my hair again. "I read in one of those books that breast-feeding will help you lose the weight faster."

"I read that, too," Stacy said, "but obviously it's not working. And now my boobs hurt." She pulled on a pair of sweats from a pile on the floor and ran a brush through her bleached hair so hard that I could hear the bristles yanking follicles out of her skull. "So where are you applying? Maybe you should wait until Safeway has openings. I bet we could get you a job there, maybe next month."

"Maybe. I want to see if I can find something sooner."

She noticed a stain on her sweats and swore, taking them off and looking for something else to wear. April started whining and reached out toward Stacy.

"I can't believe this. There's not one clean thing in here that fits me." She put the stained sweats back on and went to the mirror: black eyeliner, check; black mascara, check. Just like she used to do in the girls' room at T.N. Only now a wet spot appeared on the front of her T-shirt. "Dammit. I'm leaking. *Again*." She changed her shirt and looked at me. "I hope you know how lucky you are that Tommy didn't get you pregnant."

I did know. We hardly ever used anything. After Dad caught me, my mom dragged me to the doctor to put me on the pill, and after that we went straight to the drugstore where she bought a box of condoms. She shoved the bag into my hands without a word. She didn't need to worry. I was done with sex for a while and still had the box of condoms in my dresser drawer, unopened.

"I can do some laundry while you're at the doctor," I said. April's whining turned to crying and she squirmed around in my arms.

Stacy took April and sat down to nurse. "I don't know why I even bother getting dressed. I always look like hell anyway." She winced and looked down at April feeding. "God, kid. You don't have to suck *that* hard."

The funny thing about babies is that you know they're harmless and innocent, but sometimes they seem to be purposely making things difficult. Like April; she could be so sweet, but when she wasn't and all she did was fuss and cry, you wished you could ask her why and get her to stop. If *I* felt like that with April sometimes, it must have been a hundred times worse for Stacy. Or maybe not. Maybe if you were the mom it all seemed okay. But there were days I would look at Stacy and see how tired she was and wonder if she could really do it. Which was another reason for my plan to save up and move us all in together in our own place. Stacy and Darren and April, they needed me. I'd be like Stacy's right arm, Aunt Deanna, always there to take over when things got too hard, even for tough Stacy.

But first, I needed money. "I'll be around later if you need any help," I said, squeezing April's fat little leg before I headed out.

Lee sat on the wooden bench outside the donut shop, wearing Jason's black Metallica hoodie, leaning with her chin in her hands the way she always did. That feeling came again, like when I'd see them in the hall together at school. The hoodie meant there had been a moment: Lee and Jason alone, the sweatshirt changing hands. Did he give it to her? Did she ask him for it? Did she pretend to be cold, wrapping her arms around herself, so that he'd offer it?

She stood up and gave me a hug and I felt like crap for thinking that stuff, for being anything other than happy that they were happy. Lee is a hugger, and you can't really stay mad at a hugger. I'd never had a friend like that before. Jason isn't the type to hug anyone he isn't dating; neither is Darren. My mom is hardly ever home because of working so much and I don't think Dad has touched me since puberty, even before Tommy. Lee's mom, who I see, like, twice a month, hugs me more than anyone in my own family.

I pulled my jacket tighter around me. "I bet you at least saw the sun in Santa Barbara," I said. "It's like fifty degrees out here."

"Ah, summer in Pathetica!"

You'd think the fact that Pacifica is only about twenty miles away from San Francisco would make it cool or at least interesting, but all it is is foggy and lame and ten years behind the city in clothes and music. If you didn't get out after Terra Nova, you'd probably be stuck here your whole life, pumping gas or working at the video store or bagging at Safeway, until you'd forget there was this whole other world just fifteen minutes away.

We went in and got hit with that wave of bakery warmth and sugar and vanilla that's so incredibly good for about twenty seconds, after which point it starts to make you sick. The place was always empty except for one table in the middle, surrounded by old men in canvas hats and pastel jackets, complaining about everything, and I mean *everything*, from how no one knew how to talk about politics anymore without starting a war, to how women didn't know how to act like women anymore, to how no one knew how to make a decent donut anymore. Apparently the world was perfect in 1958.

We ate on the bench outside so the old guys wouldn't hear every word we said and start complaining about how young people today don't know how to use the English language.

"That donut was, like, two cents in the good old days," I said in a cranky old man voice.

"I have no complaint with my twenty-first–century donut," Lee said.

Caitlin Spinelli pulled into the mall parking lot and drove by us in her new Jetta, with the window down. "Must be nice," I said, watching her head bob to a rap song cranked to ten on her stereo. "She does realize that she's white, right?"

"Jettas and rap music," Lee said, "the perennial favorite of the suburban oxymoron. My first car will probably be my step-dad's El Camino. Now that's a car you can rap in."

I finished off my chocolate old-fashioned and showed my teeth to Lee. "Any chocolate droppings?"

"Nope. You're frosting free. You look nice," she said, getting up. "Like a serious job applicant."

"That's good. Because I feel like a loser." I'd dressed like some kind of conservative sorority girl in black pants and an actual blouse instead of my usual jeans and T-shirt. Suddenly I was nervous. I didn't know how it worked, this whole being hireable thing. Like, how do you convince someone you're not going to steal everything or drive away customers? This had to work; I didn't have time to waste.

We stopped at Walgreens first and I handed my application to a skinny young guy at the register.

"Someone will call you to set up an interview," he said, glancing at the application. He started to turn back to his register. "Wait. Deanna Lambert . . . I know that name."

Right, I thought. Which version of Deanna Lambert do you think you know? "When will they call me?"

He studied my face and I felt the donut in my stomach like a rock. I didn't recognize him from school, but he could have been some nameless geek from Tommy's year.

"We get a lot of applications," he said. "It might be a week. Do you go to Terra Nova?"

"Yeah," Lee said, her voice startling me. "Hey, I think you

were in my drama class last year, right?" Lee didn't even go to Terra Nova then.

"I never took drama," he said, staring at me.

Lee leaned over the counter and got louder. "Were you on the swim team?"

"Can you just put on there for them to call me as soon as possible?" I grabbed Lee's arm. "Let's *go*."

When we got outside, she said, "Okay, next?"

"He knew about me. I could tell."

"You're paranoid." She pulled me along past the boarded-up stationery store, and the shoe place that had been having a going-out-of-business sale since I was in sixth grade. Lee lowered her voice to say, "One of these days you should just look one of them in the eye and say, yeah, that's me, and so what? At my school in San Francisco, no one would even care."

"Yeah, well, this is Pacifica. One high school, one grapevine, one feature story: me."

"What about Dax Leonard getting caught with that love letter to Madame Rodriguez in French?"

I shook my head. "Not the same. Nothing actually happened. Besides, he's a guy and she's a hot teacher. If something *had* happened, he'd be a hero. Not a slut."

"Okay. Coach Waters finding Julie Archer and Tucker Bradford in the girls' locker room on Celebrate Abstinence Day. That was back in October and people are still talking about it."

"You don't get it," I said. "Julie is, like, *proud* of that story. She tells it as much as Tucker."

"I know. Sorry. I know you don't like to talk about it."

I'd already detached from the conversation. In my head I saw the girl on the waves, bobbing along, thinking my thoughts, feeling my feelings, swimming away.

A lady at Subway took my application and asked if I had any experience, as if making sandwiches was rocket science or something. After one minute in Wendy's watching the manager yell at an employee about cleaning the bathroom, I decided not to apply.

"This sucks," I said. "I want another donut."

"There's still Picasso's," Lee said, straightening my hair. "*Then* you can have another donut."

We walked over to Picasso's Pizza, this complete dump that's been at Beach Front longer than anything else. It's the last pizza place in town that isn't part of a chain, and they don't deliver, and it's basically a hangout for twenty-five-year-old guys whose primary transportation is a BMX bike.

I stared through the grease-streaked window. "I don't want to work in this hell-hole."

"Ask for the manager," Lee said. "If they ask about cashier experience, tell them you always get good grades in math and you're a fast learner."

"Now you're the expert in getting jobs? All you ever do is babysit."

"I'm just saying that's what *I'd* do."

Darren was always telling me that I should listen to Lee. She's a good girl, he'd say.

We went in. The place was always just this side of pitch-black. I don't know if that was about creating "atmosphere" or about an unpaid electricity bill. Whatever it was, we stumbled around for ten seconds before our eyes adjusted. The only person inside as far as I could see was a lady with a bad perm, stocking the salad bar with slimy-looking kidney beans. "Hi," I said, trying to sound perky and non-Deanna-like. "Is the manager here?"

"Hold on." She went into a back room and came out, a man following behind her. He was in his forties maybe, balding and thin, with a mustache. His handshake was strong, but not one of those bone-crushing shakes you get from some people who are trying to convince you of how confident they are.

"Hello," he said in a voice so deep I almost laughed. "I'm Michael."

"Hi. I'm here to drop off my job application?"

"Great. Follow me."

I turned to Lee. "Be right back."

Michael led me to a booth, my shoes making gross sticking noises as we walked across the terminally unmopped floor around the salad bar. While Michael took a pair of glasses out of his shirt pocket, I quickly grabbed a napkin and swept it over the orange vinyl of the seat, just in case.

"I should tell you," Michael said, "business is a little slow these days. Since 9/11 and Enron and Iraq and all of the other bullshit — excuse me — this country has been through, it turns out pizza doesn't hold the esteemed position in the family budget it once did."

I wanted to say that the slowdown probably had more to do with his crappy pizza and no-delivery policy than world politics, but since Picasso's was probably my last resort I kept my mouth shut.

He asked me a bunch of questions and then said, "Normally I only have two or three people working, including me. Things pick up a little in the summer and I like to have an extra person on board in case it gets busy." He paused like I was supposed to react to that.

"Uh-huh."

"Well, no one else has really applied. So." He opened up his hands and shrugged.

"What's the pay?"

"Everyone starts at minimum wage, but if you're still around after two weeks, I bump you up fifty cents. You also get a free pizza for every shift you work."

Minimum wage. That was like, nothing. The pile of money I'd be able to throw onto Darren and Stacy's bed shrunk in my mind. "How many hours a week can I get?"

"I can give you about twenty-five right now. Maybe more if someone gets sick or we get busy."

It wasn't exactly my dream job, but Michael seemed cool, like a regular no-b.s. kind of person.

"Okay," I said.

"Okay? You want the job?"

I nodded. "Sure."

Michael smiled. His teeth were yellowish, like maybe he smoked three packs a day or drank gallons of coffee.

"Terrif." He stood and shook my hand again. "Come in at six tomorrow and we'll get you started. I'll give you a Picasso's shirt then. What are you, a small?"

"Medium."

"Jeans are fine. Just make sure to put your hair back."

"Thank you," I said. Michael disappeared into the back and I found Lee. "I got it."

"Yay!" I gave her a look and she changed her tone. "I mean, 'Yay?'"

"Not really. But that's life."

"Do you get free pizza?"

"Yeah."

"Sweet!"

Stacy and my dad were arguing when I got home. They stood in the dim hall, my dad dripping wet in his robe, Stacy still wearing the dirty sweats and bouncing April in her arms. They didn't seem to notice me.

"It would be nice to have a hot shower in my own house once in a while," Dad said.

"At least *you* have *time* to shower."

"You have the same twenty-four hours in the day as everyone else." He went into the bathroom and shut the door before

Stacy could respond. I watched her stand there, staring at the spot where he'd stood. I knew that feeling.

"Hey," I said softly.

She turned, startled. "Deanna, hi."

Then she did her move.

Stacy has this thing she does, this move. No matter what's going on, she can pull herself together by giving her hair a shake and putting her right hand on her hip in this certain way, and it's, like, holy crap, don't mess with that girl. That's the girl prowling around Terra Nova, daring anyone to look at her twice. I saw her do that move after Darren's ex, Becky, shoved her down a couple of stairs at the Taco Bell at the beach. She did it the day she moved into our house, when her mom dropped her off and said, "Well, this is just about how I thought your life would turn out."

I needed a move like that.

April started to whimper. Stacy jiggled her a little as we went into the kitchen. "I committed the cardinal sin of doing my laundry. I guess there's no hot water for his shower. Oh well!" She handed April to me and got a diet soda out of the fridge. "I have to leave, like, *now* if I want to catch the bus for her appointment."

"Darren has the car?"

"Yes."

"How come you didn't just drive him to work this morning so you'd have it?"

"Well, Deanna, I guess I'm just a stupid, irresponsible, air-headed bad mother." April had gone into a full-on wail. Stacy closed her eyes. "God! Why can't she go *one* day without crying?"

I bounced April in my arms. "Um, because she's a baby?"

"You know what, Deanna? I'm glad you can be a smart-ass about it, really."

"Sorry," I said. An image flashed in my mind: Stacy in a different living room, with a nicer, ungreen carpet, and a real painting of a lighthouse over the fireplace. "We won't live here forever, Stacy."

She looked at me.

I corrected myself. "I mean, *you* won't live here forever. You and Darren and April. And I won't either." It was too soon, not the right time. "I just mean . . . someday, we'll all be gone."

"I hope so." She took April from me and headed for the front door. "I don't even know if I can make it through today."

Jason and Lee invited me to go out with them that night. Which was nice, you know, because Lee's parents only let her go out two nights a week. I should have said no, should have given them some time to themselves since Lee had been away a few days, but of course I jumped on the chance to get out of the house.

Lee's mom drove us into the city, to Stonestown, this semi-upscale mall near San Francisco State where you could wander around and usually not get jacked by wannabe gangster kids. Lee sat in the front with her mom, leaving me and Jason together in the back of the station wagon, which felt kind of funny. To me, anyway.

We pulled up to Nordstrom and Lee's mom told us to meet her back there at nine. Nine. That's Lee's curfew. In the summer! She didn't even attempt to argue.

When her mom drove off, Lee said, "Okay, who has money?"

"Not me," I said.

Jason reached into his pocket. "I got five bucks."

"I have four," Lee said, pulling ones out of her purse. "That's nine, so . . . three for each of us. Woo-hoo!" She led us into Nordy's, waving the bills, shouting, "Stand back people, we have some shopping to do!"

"Note how the salespeople are not flocking to us," Jason whispered to me, his arm brushing against mine as Lee forged ahead, laughing.

I snorted. "More like calling security."

Lee turned back, her eyes bright, a giggle still in her voice. "Come on, you guys, don't lag. We only have two hours in which to spend our fortune." She reached out her hand and Jason jogged a few steps to catch up and take it. I felt myself slowing down, pretending to look at a rack of jeans while they cuddled into one another.

Forty-five minutes into our window-shopping, we'd had enough of shuffling along the marblesque floors and watching yuppie couples buy stuff we would never be able to afford, and I couldn't help but think I should have stayed home. I'd watched Lee and Jason with their hands in each other's back pockets, like it was just that easy to be a couple, or sending each other little messages with their eyes: *You're so cute,* or *You make me smile,* or *I like the way you do that.* Or maybe they were saying: *Too bad we're not alone.*

"I might be able to buy half an earring someday," Lee said, looking at the hundredth jewelry display of the night. "If it was on sale."

"Dude," Jason said, draping his arm over her shoulder, "can we sit down already?"

"Aww. I love it when you call me 'dude.' He's such a romantic, huh, Deanna?"

"Yeah," I said, trying to sound fun and light, breezy, like her. "It's real sweet."

"I gotta take a leak," Jason said. "Meet you guys at McDonald's?"

Lee sighed. "All roads lead to McDonald's for you, Jay." She kissed him then, running her thumb over his jaw while she let her lips linger. "See you there."

What did it feel like, I wondered, to be kissed like that right out in public? Not like some passionate tongue-wrestling thing, just a kiss to declare: *We are each other's.* I'd never been kissed like that, not by Tommy or anyone else. No one had declared me his, not for the whole world to see, anyway.

Lee and I bought nine dollars worth of food and waited for

Jason in a hard plastic booth with a sticky table. I watched the kids behind the counter taking orders, changing money, sacking up burgers, move move move, a swarm of red polo shirts. "That's gonna be me in twenty-four hours," I said.

"Only without the customers," Lee said, dunking a chicken nugget into barbecue sauce. "No one actually *eats* at Picasso's."

"It's a job. I just want money."

"We need to have, like, a giant shopping spree at the end of the summer. New clothes, new everything."

I shook my head. "I'm not wasting my money on that crap."

"What crap *are* you going to waste it on?"

Jason walked up then, and slid into the booth next to Lee, reaching across the table to help himself to the community fries. "I got you something," he said to Lee through a mouthful of food.

"You did? You were withholding funds?"

"For a good cause." He reached into his jacket pocket and pulled out a small, waxy Mrs. Fields bag. "White choco-chunk whatever. You know, that one you like."

Lee's face was so happy, so truly happy over a stupid cookie, that I had to look away. My eyes stayed on the fries while they kissed.

"Here," Lee said, "does this look like thirds?" She pushed a piece of the cookie over to me, and one to Jason. "Fair and square? Or fair and cookie shaped, I guess . . ."

"Thanks, babe," Jason said, finishing his piece in one bite.

"Yeah," I said. "Thanks." It was so easy for her. Easy to be a girlfriend, easy to be a friend, easy to be a "good girl," like Darren said.

"So back to the money thing," Lee said, "your plans for your colossal summer earnings."

"You gonna buy a car?" Jason asked. "Don't do it without talking to me first."

I shook my head, not sure if I should tell them. It still felt too personal, but there I was, empty-handed, contributing nothing but my sarcastic comments and private jealousy to the whole night out. Just Deanna, the problem child, with no money or boyfriend or plans.

"I'm moving out."

Lee put her hand over her mouth.

"What do you mean you're moving out?" Jason said.

"I'm moving out. Me and Darren and Stacy." I broke a small piece out of my third of the cookie. "We're taking April at the end of the summer and getting a place."

"Seriously," Lee said. "*Seriously*? Do your parents know?"

I felt Jason's eyes on me, his bullshit detector set to high.

"Well, it's not, like, an official plan yet or anything." I was already sorry I'd said it. The words coming out of my own mouth sounded like b.s. even to me. "I kind of want to wait and see how my job goes," I said, like, no big deal, I didn't care. "If I like it, I mean, and if I make some okay money."

"Wow," Lee said. "That's huge."

"It's just an idea." I crumpled up our garbage and piled it onto a tray. "It might not even happen."

"You'd have to keep working through the whole school year, right? Like to pay your share of the rent?"

"I don't know," I said, looking at my watch. "Don't say anything. Darren and Stacy don't want it getting back to my parents."

"Right," Jason said, nodding slowly. I couldn't look at him.

I stood. "Come on," I said to Lee. "Your mom is going to be waiting."

Later that night, alone in my room, I worked on my journal. It was the only way I could stop thinking about Jason and Lee, stop thinking about how I'd opened my big, stupid mouth about the plan.

The girl in my story was still on the sea, bobbing along on her surfboard, remembering:

> . . . *sharing a pink brick of popcorn with her father at*
> *Stowe Lake: he broke off pieces with his hands; she liked*
> *to bite right into the whole thing, little bits of the candy*
> *coating sticking to her lips.*

This was my memory, I think. I remember going to the lake. I remember pink popcorn. I don't know if those things happened at the same time, or if my father was even really there.

> . . . *the smell of eucalyptus leaves crushed in her fingers.*

A different day at the park; this had happened, for sure. I still had some dried eucalyptus in my sock drawer.

. . . special slick paper he brought home so that she could draw with her markers, making colored streaks and squiggles across the shiny white.

The small declaration it made, having the surplus from National Paper, paper that traveled from Dad's office to our house to my room, from his hands and into mine: *We are each other's.*

I heard Darren come in the house; I closed my comp book. By the time he knocked on my door, I was propped up in bed reading a magazine, the girl on the waves drifting away. "Come in."

He flopped down onto the floor, stretching out on his stomach and sighing one of those after-work sighs that means you're glad the day is finally over. "Got any food in here?"

"Yeah," I said, not moving. "Let me get you a menu. How was work?"

"Oh, you know," he said into the carpet. "Same shit, different day."

Darren looks almost exactly like my dad — same dirty-blond hair; same compact, muscular body; same voice. Same temper, sometimes — only when Darren gets mad it's for good reasons, I think, like a shift at work getting screwed up or having to deal with bad drivers. He's a good brother. A good father, too, so far.

I put my magazine down. "I got a job."

"Yeah?" He rolled over onto his back, rubbing his stomach. "Good for you. You can start saving up for college."

He was always on me about getting into college. It didn't seem like reality to me, but I played along. "I've got two more summers."

"Deanna, I'm serious. I don't want you stuck in Pacifica after you graduate, hanging around and getting into trouble."

"You sound like Dad."

"No, I don't."

"Yeah, you do."

"Okay. But did you hear me?"

"Yes," I said. "You don't want me to get pregnant and not go to college and live in Mom and Dad's basement and work at Safeway my whole life. Like you and Stacy. You only tell me that fifty times a day."

He wiped his hands over his face. "Sorry. It's just that it's not too late for you, you know. You can still pull this one out."

One of the things Darren and me have in common is that we both let Mom and Dad down. Him because of having a kid so young, not to mention getting busted for pot when he was sixteen and having to go through this whole court thing. And me because, well, no one wants the school slut for a daughter. Technically, I'm not a slut, because there was only ever Tommy, but it's hard to defend myself on a technicality when things happened the way they did. It's not like I could get on the school PA system and issue a rebuttal.

Darren's cell rang. "Hey, babe," he said into the phone. "Yep. On my way." He got up. "Gotta run. Come downstairs later and watch *Letterman* with us."

"I'll have to check my calendar. Let's see," I said, squeezing my eyes shut, "yeah, looks clear."

3

I woke up early on Sunday, nervous about my first day of work. I was lying there, sort of drifting in and out of sleep, when Mom came in without knocking.

"I was thinking about French toast," she said. "How about it?"

I squinted at her. She wore her big, fuzzy pink robe, with the coffee stain on the front. "Aren't you working today?"

"They asked people to volunteer for some days off." She started straightening up my room, picking up laundry and stacking CD cases. "Don't ever work in retail." It was a funny thing to say, considering everyone in our family basically worked retail: Dad as a warehouse guy for the auto-parts supply store, Mom at Mervyns, and Darren and Stacy at Safeway. Except Dad still thought of his job at the auto place as temporary. Before that, he'd worked for National Paper for nineteen years, his first and only job until the day they laid him off.

"What about making pizzas?" I asked.

"What about it?"

"I got a job. At Picasso's."

"Clean or dirty?" she asked, holding up one of my sweatshirts, before registering what I'd said. "A job? I didn't know you were looking for a job."

"Dirty," I said. She tossed the shirt into the laundry basket. "You don't have to clean my room, Mom."

"When did you decide to get a job?"

"Isn't that what people do when they turn sixteen — work? I want to have my own money." I sat up in bed and watched her kneel on the floor near my stereo, looking for CDs to match the empty cases she'd found. About an inch and a half of gray roots showed under the auburn dye she always used.

"I wish you'd told me. Maybe I could have gotten you something at Mervyns."

"*Mom,* could you please stop touching my stuff?" I got up and took the CD cases from her. My room, which had seemed plenty big for me and Darren the night before, was way too small for me and my mom to be in together.

She looked at her empty hands. "Does your father know?"

I put a CD in its case. "I didn't know I had to ask permission."

"Well." She went over to the mirror on my closet door and frowned, fussing with her hair, pulling her bangs back with a clip from my dresser. "Most people your age would ask, wouldn't they. But you and Darren . . ." Her voice trailed off and she took the clip out. "You've always just done what you wanted."

"Mom, I thought I'd get a job is all. It's not like a tattoo or a car."

"No, you're right. It's just a job." She turned around and gave me a strained smile. "So, French toast? I never get a chance to cook Sunday breakfast for you kids. My mother would roll in her grave if she knew I work on Sundays while you all stay home and eat Pop-Tarts, not one of us in church."

Mom grew up Catholic, went to Catholic school in Daly City, the whole bit. Now we're heathens like everyone else I know. Except for Lee. Lee's family is heavy into church. Like, they go every single week. I mean, she's not like some of the kids at school who are all *What would Jesus do?* when deciding who to ask to the prom, but Lee really believes in that stuff. She just doesn't talk about it all the time.

Sometimes I wish she *would* talk about it, because I'm curious. Like, what does she say when she prays, and does she ever get mad at God? But I feel funny asking that kind of stuff; it seems so personal.

When my dad got laid off and Darren got in trouble, Mom thought maybe we needed to go to church and get right with God. She wouldn't step foot in a Catholic church for some reason, so this one Sunday we went to the Presbyterian church on the other side of town and sat near the back. It was amazing, at first: the organ music, and the morning light coming through the stained glass, and the old wood pews with their spongy, red velvet cushions.

Then some guy in a suit stood up in the front to give announcements and welcome everyone, and he asked if anyone was there for the first time. I knew from the way Mom and Dad were sort of looking down that we weren't going to get up, but an old lady behind us raised her hand and pointed us out. Dad made us all stand and said, "We're just visiting. From out of town." But there was a girl from one of my classes a couple of rows ahead of us and she looked at me funny and whispered something to her mom and I knew we'd never be back. We'd only been in the building ten minutes and already we'd lied in front of two hundred people, not to mention God.

As soon as the service was over, Mom hustled us out the side door before anyone could talk to us. In the car, Darren nudged me and showed me his open jacket pocket. He'd managed to stuff it full of cookies on our way out. So all I really remember about church is that we lied and stole and never went back. We didn't belong in church anyway. It was okay for people like Lee, people who were good and could go and believe in it and pray and not wonder if anyone was listening.

Anyway, if we didn't have church, at least we could have French toast.

I followed Mom into the kitchen. Darren sat at the table with April, holding her in his arms and giving her a bottle. She kicked her legs a little when she saw me, which always made me smile, then focused on eating.

"Where's Stacy?" I asked.

"Sleeping."

Dad appeared in the doorway in an olive green T-shirt tucked into his jeans. Even from across the room he smelled soapy from the shower. He looked young and handsome, like Darren's older brother instead of his dad. It took me by surprise and for a second it was like I was back to being seven or eight when he would give me bear hugs and tell me his favorite joke.

Hey, kiddo, how 'bout it? Did you hear the one about the two snails crossing the road?

I would laugh. Giggle. *Only ten thousand times, Dad.*

One got run over by a turtle, and when the cops questioned the other snail about what he saw, he said . . .

I'd finish the joke: *I don't know, officer, it all happened so fast.*

With him standing there in the kitchen door it was easy to think he could do it again, be that dad: pink popcorn and eucalyptus. He caught my eye and looked away. "It's after ten o'clock," he said. "Stacy should be up."

"She was up at five with the baby, Dad," Darren said. "She deserves to sleep in."

Dad got his National Paper mug down, poured himself a cup of coffee, and leaned against the counter. "What, she wants a reward for being a decent mother? Getting up with the baby is just part of the deal when you decide to get pregnant." Like Stacy just up and decided, *Gee, I think I'll get pregnant to-*

day. It would be fun, and as a bonus it would really piss off Darren's dad.

"Okay," Mom said, "who wants bacon with their French toast?"

"Me," I said.

"Me, too," said Darren.

Mom turned to Dad and held up the package of bacon. "Ray?"

"I hope you're not going out of your way to cook anything for Stacy," Dad said. "This isn't a hotel; we don't do room service."

I doubted a hotel would have a kitchen painted pink.

Darren took the bottle out of April's mouth and stood up. "Forget it. We'll go out for breakfast."

"Oh no you don't. Not after your mother has already cooked for you."

"It's all right, Ray, I haven't really started."

"No, it's not all right."

I kept my mouth shut. I didn't get involved in their fights. It's pointless, and anyway, if I take sides my dad starts saying everyone is against him and it just makes things worse.

Darren, on the other hand, has no trouble taking sides. He went over and stood by Mom. "Don't be like that to Mom just because you hate Stacy."

"Excuse me," said Dad, "for wanting better things for you than . . . *this.*" When he said "this" he sort of waved his hand around the entire kitchen, including all of us in what he obviously thought was one giant failure.

Mom stared at the package of bacon in her hands, as if still wondering how many slices to cook. Stacy walked into the kitchen in the shorts and tank top she'd slept in, went straight to the coffee pot, and filled a cup before noticing that no one besides April had moved since she came in. "What'd I miss?"

Mom managed a smile in Stacy's direction. "Would you like bacon?"

"Never mind, Mom," Darren said. He walked to Stacy. "We're going out for breakfast."

"We are?"

"Come on, Deanna."

I followed them out, avoiding Mom's eyes because this was the one flaw in my big plan: Mom would be left behind. I could see it all like a movie on a screen: her, alone with Dad for the rest of their lives, the house staying exactly the same (down to the last detail), shabby and worn-out, all the stains and holes and leaks showing, green shag carpet forever. Maybe she was an innocent bystander, like those people you read about, standing around minding their own business when the stray bullet shoots them exactly through the heart. Or maybe not so innocent. It didn't matter. In the end, she'd be the one left to walk through that door every day and try to figure out what went wrong.

Michael stood just inside Picasso's, waiting for me.

"Am I late?" I asked.

"Nope. Right on time," he said, surprising me again with his professional wrestler voice in a skinny body. We moved into the dark of the main dining area. "It's dead right now so I had nothing better to do than wait."

"Does it *ever* get busy?"

"Oh, sure. We have our regulars. Follow me; we have some paperwork to fill out and I'll give you your shirt." He led me past the counter, where I could barely make out the outline of a tall guy in a Picasso's shirt, leaning near the register. Something about the way he stood, loose and lanky, seemed familiar. My eyes started to adjust. "Oh," Michael said, "this is Tommy, your partner in crime."

"Hey, Dee Dee."

It was Tommy. My Tommy. Tommy Webber. He still had the same scruffy, dark hair and lean, tall body. Michael looked surprised. "You two know each other?"

Tommy smirked, in that way only Tommy has. "In the biblical sense."

And only Tommy would say something like that to his boss. My stomach churned; Michael raised his eyebrows. "Ahem. Okay, well then. This way, Deanna." He gestured to a booth in the back. There were some file folders on the table, a coffee cup that looked like it had never been washed, and an ashtray. He grabbed the cup. "Step into my office. Coffee? Soda?"

"I'll take a root beer," I said, trying to keep my voice steady. I sat in the booth, head spinning. Michael came back with my soda and a fresh cup of coffee for him. He took a pack of cigarettes out of his shirt pocket, tapped one out, and lit it. I watched him take a long drag and imagined how good the smoke would feel going down my own throat and into my lungs. Michael expelled the smoke with a sigh. "Good God, I needed that."

"I quit in January," I said. "I started when I was twelve."

"Good for you. For quitting, I mean. It's on my to-do list."

Right before April was born, Darren and I quit together. He bought us a box of nicotine patches, which I wore on my butt so no one would see. I wanted a smoke at that moment, though, and it agitated me to watch Michael enjoy his. "Isn't that illegal?" I said. "Smoking in a restaurant?"

"Well, yes."

I stared into my root beer, watched the little bubbles jump around on the surface. "I don't think I can work here." I said it as softly as possible so Tommy wouldn't hear me.

"What? Don't say that!" He stubbed out his cigarette. "Look, I'll stop. I won't smoke when you're here."

"It's not that."

"Oh." He looked at the perfectly good cigarette he had just ruined.

"Is Tommy here every night?"

"Well, it's usually either Tommy or Brenda. But Brenda mostly works days." Michael sighed and lit another smoke. "Is it really a problem? Was it a recent breakup?" He leaned forward and talked low, more like a gossiping teenager than a middle-aged boss. "You're too young to have a past."

If he only knew. "It was like three years ago."

"Three years? That would make you . . ." He opened a file and looked at my application. "You dated Tommy when you were *thirteen*? Isn't he out of high school?" His expression changed from surprise to concern. "Isn't that . . . a felony?"

"Yeah," I said, not specifying what I was saying yes to. And I wouldn't exactly call it dating. Tommy would show up sometimes to pick me up from junior high in the Buick — a '77 Riviera that he treated nicer than he did any of his friends — and drive me down to Half Moon Bay. We'd get stoned on the beach and mess around. It's not like he ever called me or took me other places. As for the felony thing, my dad knew he could press charges, but it was clear from the beginning that was never going to happen because it would mean talking about it. Talking about it was something he could never do.

Michael took another long drag and watched Tommy over my shoulder. "He's always on time. The register is never short. He spends half his paycheck on the Ninja Warrior machine and pizza. I'm practically *making* money off of him."

I sipped my root beer and studied the ashtray. "I don't know."

"Deanna," he pleaded, "I need you. I need someone who's not going to help themselves to the beer or call Europe from my phone. You seem normal."

"I do?"

Where else was I going to find a job in Pacifica? I wished I had a car, or at least a driver's license. There were probably a zillion jobs in the city, where there would be no Tommy. But it wasn't like I had all the time in the world. If there wasn't a real stack of cash to show Darren and Stacy at the end of the summer, I'd have nothing to offer them. The last thing they needed was my deadweight. They wouldn't need me, they wouldn't want me, they wouldn't take me, and I'd be stuck in that house alone, belonging to no one.

I watched Michael watching me. If he was going to be around most of the time, it might be okay. He seemed like the kind of person I could trust. He took another drag of his smoke and it hit me — something about the way he flicked his ash or the way he was talking to me in hushed tones like a girlfriend — Michael was gay. For some reason that made me feel better, like maybe he'd be on my side. "You don't even have to be nice to Tommy," he said. "I'm usually around here anyway. I have no life. I'll keep an eye out for you."

"That's okay," I said. "I can handle him." I didn't know if that was the truth. The only thing I knew was that I needed the money.

"You're going to stay? Oh thank God." He pulled some papers out of his file. "Let's do your W-4 and emergency form, then I'll get you started, okay?"

"Okay."

I managed to avoid Tommy most of the night, staying by Michael's side while he showed me how to make a pizza (harder than it looks), how to run the dishwasher (not exactly brain surgery), where we kept stuff in the walk-in refrigerator (a.k.a.

a disorganized mess), how to stock the salad bar (moldy side down), and how to run the slicer (*without* cutting off your hand). When he got a phone call and disappeared into the back room to take it, I busied myself wiping down the salad bar and all the tables.

Tommy leaned on the cash register and watched me. "You're not even going to say hi to me, Dee Dee?"

His voice shot through me. It's amazing, the things your body will do just when you don't want them to: heart speeding up, fingers aching. I'd always liked his voice, low and laid-back, the kind of voice that made you listen, a voice that still caused me to teeter when I heard it saying my old nickname.

"Nobody calls me that anymore," I said.

"I do."

A declaration.

"Well, don't."

"Okay, Dee Dee."

I went to the back and into the walk-in, where I sat on a bucket of sliced tomatoes. It was cold in there, obviously, but quiet. I could think. It's not like I hadn't seen Tommy since that night with my dad; I'd seen him driving around a couple of times, and once at a party. But those times were more like seeing a vision or something out of a dream. Here he was, living and walking and talking — talking to me like he used to, calling me Dee Dee.

Come on, Dee Dee. Come on. I remembered exactly how it felt when he wrapped my ponytail around his hand, pulling it back until I got the hint that he wanted me to go down. *Come on.* He said doing that wasn't really sex, that I'd still be a virgin. Then after a while, being a virgin somehow didn't matter so much.

My hair was in a ponytail now because Michael said it had to be up. I tucked it into a bun and went back out into the dim restaurant.

"Oh, there you are," Michael said. "We've got customers. Go ahead and help Tommy with the pizzas."

I grabbed a pizza crust and joined Tommy at the counter. He glanced at me and smiled. "Where's your ponytail, Dee Dee?"

Something in me surged again, and I should have told him to go to hell but I didn't want to give him anything, not one single hint that he could still make me feel things, even hate.

Michael waited outside with me after Tommy left. Darren was supposed to pick me up at eleven thirty; at ten to midnight he still hadn't showed. There were maybe eight cars left in the entire Beach Front lot, fog creeping in over the asphalt.

"I'm about to turn into a pumpkin," Michael said, checking his watch. "Do you need a lift?"

"He'll be here. You don't have to wait."

Michael sucked on his cigarette. The man was a nicotine fiend. "So, was it awful? Are you going to come back?"

"I need the money."

He nodded. "Why else would anyone work here? I know it's a dive, but it's *my* dive."

Darren's Nova pulled into the lot. "There he is."

Michael patted me on the shoulder. "Okay, see you tomorrow."

I got in the car and as soon as I closed the door, Darren asked, "Who's that guy?"

"Michael, my boss."

"He's after you already?"

"God, Darren." Ever since Tommy, Darren was a little on the overprotective side, always watching guys watching me, more than once threatening to kick the ass of anyone who looked at me too long.

"Well? I mean, if it's gonna be like that you should just quit right now."

"He's gay."

"Oh." Darren glanced in the rearview mirror to watch Michael getting into his Toyota. "How come he's touching you, then?"

"Because he's nice. It's called affection. You may have heard of it? Anyway, if you were on time, he wouldn't *have* to wait with me." It was sort of funny how suspicious Darren was of Michael, given the fact that if he knew Tommy worked there he'd shit himself.

"Yeah, yeah, smart-ass," he said. "Stacy can get you from now on, straight from work. So how was it? Where's my free pizza?"

"I ate *my* free pizza on my break. Work was okay."

"You stink like onions."

"I know. It's gross." There was tomato sauce under my nails and this greasy film all over me and I reeked like the inside of the pizza oven. "What'd you guys do today?"

"We drove into the city and shopped for some clothes for Stacy and hung out at the beach for a while. Looked at some places for rent."

The smell of my own pizza-stink, the sound of Tommy's voice in my head, and what Darren was saying overwhelmed me all at once and I felt like I could throw up. I rolled down my window; cool air washed over me.

"I thought you guys had to save up, like, a couple thousand dollars," I said. "For first and last, and the deposit and everything."

"Yeah, basically. We're thinking about asking Stacy's mom for help."

No.

No, no, no.

If Stacy's mom helped them, they wouldn't need me.

I talked fast, like Mom did when she was nervous. "She's not going to help you. Her and Stacy have barely talked since April was born. God, why would you want anything from her anyway? You'll just owe her for, like, *ever*." I was practically yelling. I took some deep breaths and looked out the window, let the fog blow on my face and form little droplets of salty water on my skin. I felt Darren looking at me.

"Calm *down*," he said. "We probably won't ask her. All we did was talk about it."

We pulled up to the house and Darren got out. I stayed sitting in the front seat for a while, staring out at the street. All the garbage cans were out for morning pickup and a few neighborhood cats prowled around, darting from front yards to the curb, under cars, slinking across the street.

I did the math in my head. How many paychecks, how many weeks of scraping cheese off the counter, how many hours of Tommy's eyes on me would it cost to buy my way out?

Darren stuck his head in the passenger window and I jumped. "You coming in, or what?"

I got out of the car and followed him into the house: just a building I lived in while waiting for something real to happen.

I hated Mondays. Mom worked, Darren worked, and Stacy took the car to do errands, which left me home alone with Dad, who had the day off. It was bad enough during the school year when I had a couple of hours between school and dinner to kill alone with him in the house; in summer it was impossible to deal with. I had to get out.

I called Jason. I needed to tell someone about Tommy showing back up in my life. It could have been Lee that I called, but I wasn't up for the kind of pep talk I would get from her. And, okay, I knew that she was taking a pottery class with her mom on Monday mornings for the next few weeks and it was a chance for me to have Jason to myself. I pictured Lee, sliding exactly one-third of her special boyfriend cookie over to me, and felt a pang of guilt.

"Hey," I said into the phone.

"What up?"

"I need to get out."

"Okay. I don't have any money, though. You?"

"What do you think?"

"Just come over," he said, the sound of his voice calming me down already. "My mom is working from home today, but she won't bug us. She's got a Clint Eastwood marathon on TV."

"How is that 'working from home'?"

"I don't ask questions."

"I'll be there in ten."

I grabbed my jacket and tried to slip out without being noticed, but Dad was out front working on his car. He looked up. "Where are you going?"

"Jason's."

"With Lee?"

"No. Just me and Jason." I could have lied and avoided what came next, but I had nothing to hide.

Dad wiped his hands on a greasy rag and came closer. "Why?"

"Because Lee can't come."

"Why not?"

"Because she's busy."

"You can't stay home for one day?"

And do what? Sit in my room and wish I was somewhere else? "Jason's mom is going to be there."

Dad went back to the car and stuck his head under the hood. "Lee doesn't mind you being alone with Jason?"

My face got hot. Usually Dad didn't just come out and say stuff like that, stuff that told me without a doubt what he thought of me. Most of the time it was what he didn't say that hurt. I walked away without answering him, down the drive-way, down the block, toward Jason's. The farther away I got from the house, the better I felt.

His mom answered the door. "Hi, Deanna, can't talk. Clint's about to crack the case . . . Jason is in his room," she said, dart-ing back to the TV.

I walked down the hall to Jason's room, over the peach-colored carpet, a path I'd walked practically my whole life, from when it was brand new to now, a throw rug covering the spot where Jason spilled model paint in fifth grade. Jason's room has a smell, too, that's never changed. It's this citrusy, sweaty boy smell. It isn't rank or anything, just sort of dark and deep, like orange peels left in the sun.

Jason was on his bed. I sat on the floor. I imagined my dad watching us on a surveillance camera, staring in surprise as we innocently watched TV instead of making out or snorting coke or piercing each other's nipples or whatever it was my dad thought I did with my spare time.

During commercials I told him about my job, thinking that

any second I would tell the part about Tommy working there. It never quite happened. Maybe because I wasn't ready to talk about it, or maybe because just being with Jason was enough to make everything feel okay.

"*I* should get a job," he said. "On the other hand, maybe I should spend all summer sleeping and watching TV. Yeah, that sounds good."

We raided the fridge and ate leftover spaghetti and corn chips at the kitchen table. "I don't want to go home," I said.

"So don't," Jason said. "You can crash here."

I used to do that all the time when we were kids, just stay over at Jason's like he was any girlfriend, the two of us in our sleeping bags, side by side on the living room floor. We'd shine flashlights on the ceiling and get graham-cracker crumbs all over the rug.

"I don't think so."

"My mom doesn't care."

"My dad does."

He finished off his spaghetti. "I think there's some cake. Want cake?"

"Lemme think. Okay, yes."

See, that's what I needed. Not a pep talk, not a big speech about my low self-esteem, not a two-hour reliving of the whole Tommy Era. Just cake, and the familiar feel of Jason's carpet under my feet, the smell of his room, his face, the history of our friendship everywhere I looked.

4.

The next night, Tommy cornered me in the walk-in while I refilled a tub of pizza sauce. He stood right up close to me, all in my personal space. My body did things again, nerves awake, something not quite good and not quite bad creeping over my scalp.

"Hang out after closing," he said, confident, like I wouldn't say no. "I've got some burnables."

Sitting around an empty pizza place and smoking pot with him should have pretty much been my idea of hell. I should have laughed in his face. But this is what I did not expect: Near Tommy I felt thirteen again: childish and inexperienced, a little afraid and a little excited. Especially there in the closeness of the walk-in, which was too much like where I first met him.

He'd been at our house hanging out with Darren — me, in the bathroom playing with a bunch of makeup I'd just bought. The door wasn't closed all the way and Tommy walked right in on me. He leaned in the doorway so that I couldn't get out unless I pushed him out of the way, which I did not do.

"How come you're putting that crap on your face?" he asked, pointing to my little pile of drugstore eyeliner and mascara and lip gloss.

Tommy was cute. Taller than any of the boys at my junior high, definitely, with a scar on the left side of his face that gave him a tough, sort of dangerous look that I thought was cool. The main thing, though, was the way he looked at me. Like I was being seen for the first time.

"It makes me look older," I said, barely getting the words out.

Tommy looked at me in the mirror. "It makes you look trashy."

Him saying that made me feel small and dumb. I should have walked away, but at that moment I wanted more than anything for someone to keep looking at me the way he did. I stared hard at myself and decided maybe the makeup didn't look so good; not trashy like he said, but like I was trying too hard. Like a little kid playing dress up, which is basically what I was. So I washed my face while Tommy watched.

"You think guys like that," he said, "all that makeup and shit. But really, the thing that's a turn on?" I tuned into Tommy then like I'd landed on a new radio station that was going to tell me everything I'd ever wanted to know about myself. He stood behind me at the sink and we looked at each other in the mirror. The makeup was off, the hair around my face damp. "Is when a girl is clean and fresh, like she just got out of the shower. Yeah. Just like that."

When he said that, he put his hands on the sink on either side of me, with his body sort of pressed up against my back. He was warm, a kind of warm I'd never felt. And he was telling me I had something, *me,* that could actually have an effect on another person.

"See? You're real pretty now," he said in that confident, easy voice; a declaration. "Just like that."

It happened right then; he looked at me and it was the thing I'd been waiting for but didn't know it. I don't mean anything corny like I fell in love or even into a crush or anything like that. It was more a feeling like when I'd get picked first for volleyball or find one of those stupid school candygrams in my locker. It was knowing someone else thought about me for more than one second, maybe even thought about me when I wasn't there.

We stared at each other in the mirror, something crackling between us.

Then we heard Darren coming down the hall and I grabbed my makeup and pushed past Tommy to get out of the bathroom and into my room. I remember lying on my bed for a long time after that, thinking about Tommy and what he said and how he said it, the way the hard muscles in his arms were shaped as he leaned into the sink, over and over and over until I fell asleep with this warm, restless, achy feeling.

And that's how I felt again, there in the walk-in with Tommy up close, even after everything that had happened, everything I knew about who he was.

"Come on, Dee Dee," he said, his voice low. "It'll be fun. It's not like you have anything better to do, right? I know you don't have a boyfriend."

"How do you know that?"

He shrugged and smiled. "Just a hunch."

I came to my senses then. Tommy was still a jerk who thought those hours in the car with him summed up my life.

"Don't call me Dee Dee. I told you." I held the pizza sauce between us. "Stacy is picking me up at closing. If she sees you, she'll tell Darren, who will then proceed to kick your ass."

"I'm so scared."

Michael showed up outside the walk-in. "Tommy? You're supposed to be on the register. Sometime today, I'm hoping." Tommy grinned and walked out. "Is he bothering you?" Michael asked. "Tell me if he's bothering you."

"No," I said. "He's nobody."

I sat on the floor of my room, with my back against the door so no one could walk in. The comp book was open on my lap, my pen hovering over the paper.

Tommy leaning into me.

Tommy locking his eyes on mine in the mirror, declaring.

Tommy in the walk-in. His voice, his eyes, his scar, his arms. My body, his body.

This is the last time, the girl thought, that she would remember these things.

If they floated back to her again, she would paddle away.

Belonging to someone, something.

The way my dad used to look at me; the way he looked at me now.

When the remembering was done, the forgetting could begin.

5.

Lee called me the next day.

I figured it was a sign, my chance to tell her all about Tommy reappearing and everything that meant or might mean. But Lee didn't ask about my job or my day or anything about my life. She started right out with, "Hey, I need your advice."

"Okay. About what?"

"I can't talk now; my mom is lurking around here some-where. When do you have to be at work? Can we get together?"

We made plans to meet at Picasso's an hour before my shift. I should have told her right then about Tommy working there, but the words didn't come out. What if when she saw him in the flesh she thought different about what had gone on? Maybe she pictured him in her head as some studly bad boy or something, and when she saw the skinny white-trash reality she'd change her mind about things, change her mind about me.

When I got off the phone, I went into the kitchen for a root beer. Mom had just gotten home from work, and she and Dad were in the backyard. I could see and hear them through the open window.

"When was she planning to tell me?" Dad asked. He was cleaning his car tools. "When do *I* get to know what's going on around here?"

"It's a job, Ray. It's a *good* thing."

"Hanging around a strip mall at night? A good way to get in trouble, maybe."

See, he talked about me that way even when he thought I couldn't hear. It wasn't just something he did when I was around so that he could make me feel like crap, punish me, or whatever. If I needed proof about what he really thought, here it was.

"I'm sure she was planning to mention it."

"*Mention* it?" He threw a wrench onto the grass, where it clinked against another tool. "Like you *mentioned* that Stacy was pregnant three weeks after Darren told you? Don't I have a right to know what's going on in my own house?"

Don't worry, Dad. We'll all be out of your life soon enough.

"Maybe you should ask more questions, talk to them more, and they would tell you things." Mom talked fast, biting her nails. I wanted to leave the kitchen, didn't want to hear whatever else my dad was going to say about me. But I stood in my spot, motionless.

"I ask questions," Dad said.

Mom sighed. "You interrogate."

Dad threw another tool onto the pile. "You would too if you'd seen what I did."

"Ray, it was so long ago."

"Doesn't feel that way to me." Dad headed toward the house. I moved quickly into the hall so that he wouldn't see me. As he came in the back, I heard him say, "Could have been yesterday, the way it feels."

Sometimes this would happen:

I'd start reliving everything and I wouldn't be able to stop thinking what if. What if I hadn't met Tommy, or I'd been smart enough to tell him to leave me alone, or my dad hadn't followed us to Montara that night? Or if he had, what if he was the kind of dad who gave me a hug and smoothed my hair back and said, "Are you okay?"

And I'd start thinking what if all these things and I could sit there for hours, spinning it over and over in my head until tears felt like they were coming on, and I'd make myself stop.

I hate to cry. One of the last times I cried was when Tommy and I had sex for the first time, months before that night my dad found us. It hurt so much and Tommy was stoned and not even paying attention to how I tried to slow him down and there was some stupid commercial for a diet pill on the car radio. I could feel the tears sliding down the side of my face and dripping a little into my ears. But the worst part was when Tommy saw that I was crying and he got all nice and *Hey Dee Dee, don't cry, it will get better, you look so pretty . . . come on now, Dee Dee, come on.* It was like he had something on me, like he'd seen deep into somewhere he didn't belong.

But anyway, Tommy was only part of the what ifs.

What if National Paper had never laid my dad off? Would that have made it easier for him to be the other kind of father?

What if Mom didn't have to work at a department store, with people complaining all day about stuff they'd bought, or leaving piles of clothes on dressing room floors for her to pick up? Would she look so gray and tired? Would she have noticed when I stopped coming home right after school, climbing instead into Tommy's Buick and driving off for hours?

What if Darren and Stacy got married, in a regular wedding, maybe even in a church, before April was born?

What if I had more than two friends?

What if Jason had chosen me instead of Lee?

What if everyone got another chance after making a big mistake?

Lee was waiting for me in front of Picasso's like we'd planned, wearing her favorite blue pullover instead of Jason's Metallica sweatshirt. A mean part of me liked to imagine Jason saying something like, *Look, can I have my sweatshirt back once in a while?*

We went inside, enveloped by the perpetual darkness that was Picasso's. I saw the outline of Tommy, leaning on the counter, chewing a plastic straw. Other than one family in a front booth, there were no customers.

"Dee Dee," Tommy said as we got closer, "who's your friend?"

I ignored him, but Lee said, "I'm Lee," as if Tommy was some friend of her parents who actually deserved an introduction. I wondered if I could get by without telling her that he was Tommy; *the* Tommy. I went over to the fountain and scooped two cups of ice, filling them with root beer. Tommy watched.

"Why don't you make us a pizza instead of standing there looking like an asshole," I said.

Michael came out from the back, carrying a bucket of lettuce for the salad bar. "You're here early," he said to me. "It's not busy enough for me to put you on yet."

"I know. We're just here for pizza."

"Wow, a paying customer. Where have you been all my life?" He dumped the lettuce into the big bowl in the middle of the salad bar and mixed it around with the older brown lettuce that was already in there. Like no one was going to notice.

"I have to pay?"

"Well, half price when you're not working. It's better than nothing." He stirred up the other salad bar stuff to make it look more fresh, then turned to the counter. "Tommy? A half-priced pizza for the ladies."

Tommy grinned at Michael. "Oh, you're eating, too?"

· 72 ·

"Har-de-har."

I ordered a Hawaiian special for us and we took a booth.

"This seems like a fun place to work," Lee said.

"The key word is 'seems'."

There was a loud clatter from the family up front; a kid started to cry.

"That's *it*," the mom said, "no more soda."

"I didn't spill it on *purpose*," the kid wailed. "I didn't *mean* to spill it!"

I gestured toward the family. "Case in point. Now they'll use about eight-hundred napkins to clean up what's on the table while the rest soaks into the floor. Later, I'll run a dirty mop over it, only of course I won't be able to see what the hell I'm doing because Michael doesn't believe in lightbulbs. Good times."

"Still," Lee said, "at least you have, like, a rapport with your coworkers and everything."

"Is that what you call it?"

She studied me. "Are you okay?"

"Yeah." I sucked soda up the straw then let it slide back down into the glass, the way I'd done when I was a kid. "You wanted my advice?"

"Ye-es," she said slowly, "but first, are you sure you're okay? You seem . . . kinda sketchy. Not totally you. Is it about moving out this summer? Did you tell your parents? Did they freak?"

"No. They don't know about that. Like I said, it's not really a plan. Just an idea."

I should have told her then about Tommy, but he walked over with a pitcher of root beer and another chance slipped by.

"Refill?" he asked, winking at Lee.

"We *just* sat down," I said, instead of "You make me sick," which is what I really wanted to say. When he walked away, I said, "I'm fine. Bring it on. I'm here to advise you."

I watched Tommy walk over to the jukebox and slip in a few quarters. He punched up his numbers, and the first of what I knew would be a string of bad '80s rock songs blared from the machine.

Lee looked over her shoulder and laughed. "Is it always that loud?"

"Don't worry. In a second, Michael will come out and turn it down. It's a sacred ritual."

"Before I forget: We're leaving tomorrow on a family camping thing. Burt wants to start a tradition. Seems a little late for that since Peter is already in college, but . . ."

"You're leaving *tomorrow*?" She always had all this *stuff* going on in her life: church stuff and family stuff and couple stuff. "How long will you be gone?"

"Ten days, I think. If I survive that long."

I jabbed my straw into my root beer and played with the ice. "Sounds like fun."

She rolled her eyes. "I know."

"No," I said, "really, it sounds like fun. Like, a whole family going off together and doing something that's not work. Fun."

"You want me to find out if you can come?" Then she gave

me one of those Lee's Special Looks, the kind that made me feel lower than low for imagining *myself* with Jason in her place. It was the look that meant you had all her attention, that she'd drop everything to hear what was on your mind and then do anything she could to make it better. On a good day, I'd take that look and start talking. On a bad day, all I could think was that I didn't deserve it.

"I'm kidding," I said, doing my best imitation of Stacy's move. The head toss, anyway. "Advice!"

As I predicted, Michael came out of the back room and turned the jukebox down just as Tommy brought our pizza over, eyeing Lee. "Dee Dee doesn't love me anymore," he said, "but you're kind of cute. Do you have a boyfriend?"

"Shut up," I said. "She's too old for you."

When he walked away, Lee whispered, "How come you're so mean to him? He's not bad."

I tried to see him through her eyes: tall and reasonably cute, with slept-on dark hair and his easy way of flirting. Just another harmless, going-nowhere Pacifica slacker.

"It's *rapport*, like you said. Anyway, you don't know him like I do." I pulled off a piece of pizza, breaking the strings of cheese with a plastic knife. "He used to hang with Darren." Hint, hint.

She didn't get it, busy instead with getting her own piece of pizza. "Ham and pineapple. Pure genius." She took a deep breath. "Okay. It's about Jay."

The hot cheese burned my tongue. I sucked down some root beer, but it didn't taste good anymore, sticky and too sweet. I knew from her face, the way she wouldn't meet my eyes and the way she looked like she could either burst into tears or giggles, what kind of advice she wanted.

"It's about sex, right?"

She nodded, covering her face with her small hands. Her nails were never dirty. "You don't have to say it so loud."

I looked around. The family had left, Tommy was taking a phone order, and Michael was in the back. "He wants to have it and you don't, right?"

She nodded again, but wouldn't take her hands off of her face. It made me mad somehow; I wanted to shake her and tell her to stop acting like a baby. Instead, I picked at a piece of vinyl coming loose from my booth seat. "If you don't want to, then don't," I said. "It's not like Jason is going to date-rape you or something."

"I *know*. God, Deanna." She dropped her hands to the table.

"So what's the problem?" I tried to keep my feelings out of my voice, tried to act the part of the helpful best friend. "I mean, I know he didn't say he'd break up with you if you didn't. That's just not Jason."

"No, he didn't say that." She nibbled at her pizza crust; Tommy approached. "But, I don't know. Maybe I do want to."

"Want to what?" Tommy said, spinning his bar towel. "Go out with me?"

"As if I'd let her ruin her life," I said.

"You're just jealous."

"Would you please leave us the hell alone?"

"Hey, I can take a hint." Tommy bent down to look Lee in the eyes. I tore off a tiny piece of the vinyl I'd been picking at. "Come back and see me sometime."

Lee giggled. She actually *giggled.* As soon as Tommy was out of earshot, I leaned forward and said quietly but clearly, slowly: "If you can't see through a guy like Tommy, you shouldn't even be *thinking* about having sex."

She looked confused. "I'm talking about Jason, not Tommy." Her eyes got big and she glanced over her shoulder and back at me. "That's Tommy? I mean, *Tommy* Tommy?"

"Yes."

"Why didn't you *tell* me he worked here?"

"I don't know," I said, shoving the pizza pan aside, the smell of hot pineapple making me sick. "But like you said, we're not talking about Tommy. We're talking about Jason." I worked my finger into the hole I'd made in the seat and found the crumbling foam beneath.

She looked over at Tommy again. He waved and grinned from behind the counter. "So *that's* Tommy." She nodded a little. "Yeah. I can see that. How can you work here? Doesn't being around him make you feel weird? Does Darren know? I can't believe you didn't tell me!"

I don't know. Yes. No. "I was going to."

"He's not like I pictured," she said, "but I think I get it. He has, like, an *energy.*"

I didn't want to talk about it, not now, when it felt better to be mad at Lee than to have her care about my life, or worse, act like she understood it. I tore at the vinyl some more, making the hole bigger.

"Back to Jason," I said, "because I have to start my shift soon. Isn't it, like, against your religion to have sex? Before marriage, I mean?"

"Yeah, well, sort of. I don't know." She sighed. "It's *Jason.*"

Hearing his name like that, her saying it with so much affection like maybe she actually loved him, I don't know, but I wanted to knock the pizza and root beer off the table and run out of Picasso's. It wasn't fair, Lee getting to think about losing her virginity with a nice guy like Jason, someone who spent his last two bucks on her favorite cookie, someone who didn't get her stoned so he could feel her up, someone who didn't drive her to deserted parking lots without at least taking her out to a movie first. Someone who made a declaration *for* her, and not just in the backseat of a car.

I didn't want her to have that, not with Jason. I felt so third grade, like I wanted to push Lee to the ground and say *I knew him first.*

"Right," I said. "It's Jason. And it's not like you're going to marry him. I mean, eventually you either break up or marry or move in together or whatever, right? Which do you think it's going to be with Jason, honestly?"

Lee looked up at me, her face red. "You don't have to say it like that." A tear slipped out of her eye and my heart squeezed.

I wanted to take it all back and start the conversation over, but it was too late. If it had been anyone but Jason, anyone, maybe I wouldn't have made such a mess out of it, but I just kept talking, pulling little chunks of foam out of the booth seat and flinging them on the floor.

"You want my advice? My advice is that you're not missing anything and in a couple of years you'll go to college and me and Jason will be here in Pathetica working crap-ass jobs and hanging out at Denny's, so why waste your time? On either of us."

More tears. She had to take a napkin out of the dispenser and hold it up to her face. I should have gotten up, slid into the booth next to her and put my arms around her, hugging her the way she hugged me every time she saw me. I'd say I was sorry, that I was just jealous and to forget what I said. I'd ask Michael for the night off. We'd walk home together in the foggy summer night and I'd tell her about sex; the good stuff, like how it could be warm and exciting — it took you away — and the not-so-good things, like, how once you showed some- one that part of yourself, you had to trust them one thousand percent and anything could happen. Someone you thought you knew could change and suddenly not want you, suddenly decide you made a better story than a girlfriend. Or how some- times you might think you wanted to do it and then halfway through or afterward realize no, you just wanted the company, really; you wanted someone to choose you, and the sex part it- self was like a trade-off, something you felt like you had to give to get the other part. I'd tell her all that and help her decide. I'd be a friend.

I couldn't be that person, somehow, no matter how much I wanted to. She was inside me; I could see her and picture her, hear her. But who was I to *be* her? I was Deanna Lambert, eighth-grade slut forever; Tommy's funny story; my dad's biggest embarrassment. I got up and left Lee crying at the table with, "Have fun on your camping trip." I walked into the back and stayed there until I was sure she was gone.

I ignored Tommy the rest of the night, which was pretty easy because we hardly had any customers and he worked in the back, doing inventory with Michael.

After work, I waited out front for Stacy to pick me up after her shift. I said nothing in reply to Tommy's, "See ya on the flip side, Dee Dee."

Michael waited with me again, sighing his cigarette smoke into the night. "So how'd your friend like my pizza?"

I shrugged. It didn't matter; it wasn't like Lee was ever going to talk to me again.

"That good, huh?"

A beat-up Mustang roared by us and through the parking lot, chased by a newer Civic with tinted windows. I watched their headlights whip around the corner and disappear. Across the lot, outside the closed donut shop, a man and woman drank beer from cans. That would be me someday, I thought, stuck in strip mall hell, freezing my ass off in the summer and getting smashed with some Tommy-like loser who would probably be my only friend.

I turned to Michael. "Can I ask you a question?"

"Be my guest," he said.

"You're, like, an adult with freedom and money, right?"

"In theory."

"Why would you choose to live *here*?"

He laughed. "Are you kidding? I love this town!"

"*Why?*"

"It's got everything: the beach, a video store, Safeway, rent I can almost afford. It's quiet, but I can be in San Francisco in half an hour anytime I want." He swept his arm around through the damp grayness, cigarette glowing. "And the fog! Don't you love the fog?"

"If when you say 'love' you mean 'hate with a white-hot passion,' then yeah, I love the fog."

"Oh, Deanna. You're so adorably cynical." He flipped the collar of his jacket up and chuckled. "I guess it is a little chilly."

Stacy pulled up; I said good-bye to Michael and jumped in. When we got to our street, she brought the Nova to a dead stop and looked at me. "We should go out," she said. "Girls' night, you know? We never do that. Drinks and jukeboxes and acting stupid, right? You're not a kid anymore," she said, getting more excited, "we could get you a fake ID, easy. I could call Kyle Peterson . . ."

I looked at her to see if she was serious. She still had on her

Safeway smock and her hair was pinned back, no sign of the crazy Stacy she'd been when Darren first met her. "What," I said, "like, leave Darren at home with April and just go buck wild in a bar? Like that's going to be okay with him?"

"Once in a while, sure. Not every week." She lifted her hands and then let them fall back on the steering wheel with a smack. "Forget it. It's just an idea."

We sat at the corner until a car came up behind us and honked.

"Shit," she said. "I guess we're going home." She turned down the street and we pulled up to the house.

I imagined a time not too far off when she and I would be pulling up to a different house, a different door. It would be a place we'd look forward to going to. We wouldn't be able to keep from relaxing into the seats as we pointed the car toward home. In a place like that, I'd be able to reach across whatever it was that couldn't let me be the kind of friend Lee needed that night, or to be the kind of daughter my dad wanted. I'd reach across and grab the hand of that other Deanna and say come on, it's okay now. You're home.

6.

The next morning, I stayed in bed, under the covers, until Mom and Dad and Darren had left for work.

Night on the ocean was a world apart from day.
Endless dark, enough to make the bravest afraid.

The girl started to wonder if anyone would look for her.

I reread everything I'd written so far. It sucked. It all just sucked. It wasn't a story, it wasn't a journal, it wasn't a poem. It wasn't anything. I put giant X's through the pages, shoved the book behind my bed, and went downstairs to watch TV with

Stacy, feeling bad for blowing off her girls' night idea. For about three seconds I thought I might tell her about Tommy, but she would have thought it was her duty to tell Darren and the shit would hit the fan.

She sat on the floor looking through a magazine while April slept. I got into the bed, which was still warm, and scooted closer to Stacy so that I could look at the magazine over her shoulder while half watching *The Young and the Restless*.

"Jack Abbott is using some serious hair products today," I said.

"No doubt."

We sat like that for a while, reading up on celebrity dating and fashion and watching TV. I noticed Stacy's fingernails were short and ragged, with just a few chips of red from a month-old manicure. "Want me to do your nails?"

"Oh, hell yes."

I got up and rummaged around in the bag of makeup she kept under the bed. At the bottom of the bag was an old box of hair dye. "Did you know you have a perfectly good box of Copper Sunset in here?"

"Huh?"

I held up the box. "I thought you've always been a blond?"

"I have." She took the box from me and studied it. "I got this a long time ago. Thought I needed a change. Then I got pregnant and that was enough of a change for me."

"Maybe you can exchange it at the store for blond highlights or something."

Stacy was quiet, still staring at the box. "Or Darren could come home tonight and screw a redhead."

"Gross."

"Oh please. How do you think April happened?"

"I don't need a visual, thanks."

She stood up and checked on April. "She's still asleep, believe it or not." She waved the box at me. "So are you going to help me do this or what?"

"Seriously?" But I didn't have to ask. The old Stacy was there in her eyes. Before April, Stacy would try just about anything once, including running topless through the Golden Gate National Cemetery at night, and flipping off the principal on her graduation day. Maybe this is what our lives would be like when we moved out, Stacy and me like sisters, doing each other's hair and nails and sharing secrets. . . .

I followed her into the tiny basement bathroom, with the cheap peel-and-stick floor that had never been lined up right and the half-burned Christmas candle on the back of the toilet. Stacy took off her top so it wouldn't get messed up, and I mixed the dye. When I'd gotten half the bottle onto her head, she said, "Darren is going to *freak*."

"We can rinse it out right now," I said.

"No. It's just hair. Who cares?"

When I'd gotten Stacy's hair totally covered with dye, April woke up. We hung out in the bedroom, played with the baby while we waited for twenty-five minutes to tick by. "What if you hate it?" I asked.

Stacy shrugged, sitting cross-legged on the bed in her bra and jeans, dabbing polish remover onto her nails. "I already hate everything else about my life, so what's one more thing?"

I stopped playing with April and looked at Stacy. "You don't hate *everything* about your life."

"Yeah, pretty much." I wanted to ask what about Darren and April, what about me, but something stopped me. Maybe I was afraid to hear what she'd say. "Time's up," she said. "I'm gonna rinse."

I held April, looked into her eyes and saw Darren and Stacy and parts of her that were just April. She smiled at me and held onto my finger and I stopped thinking about Stacy saying she hated everything about her life. I stopped thinking about Tommy and my dad, or Lee, or Jason. All I could think about was how small April was, and how her skin was so soft and new. She was like a perfect pink little cupcake, fresh out of the oven.

"Oh my God. Come here," Stacy called from the bathroom. I put April back in her crib. When I saw Stacy I covered my mouth. Her hair was wet. And red. Well, not red, but Copper Sunset. It made her look older and more serious; it made her look smarter, like a college student or someone who worked in a bank.

"Whoa. You totally do not look like you."

She stared at herself in the mirror. She didn't seem unhappy with it. All she said was, "Yeah. I could be anyone."

When Darren got home I followed him down to the basement so I could see his reaction to Stacy's hair. I don't know why I was so excited, practically dancing down the hall, pushing him ahead of me, telling him we had a big surprise.

"What's your damage?" he asked, laughing. "Are you on something?"

"You'll see!"

Stacy stood waiting in the room, dressed head to toe in black, with heavy goth-style eye makeup and a wicked grin. "Hey, baby," she said, winking at Darren, "what's *your* name?"

I don't know how Darren turned so dumb all of a sudden, but he just kind of slipped off his Safeway jacket and said, "That looks great, babe! I've always wanted to kiss a hot redhead."

He grabbed her for a hug, playful, but she pulled away. "Don't. God."

"What?"

"That's all you can say?" She put on a fake dumb-guy voice and imitated him. *"I've always wanted to kiss a hot redhead."*

Darren backed away, holding up his hands. "What'd I do?"

"Just forget it." Stacy did her move. April started to cry. I didn't know what to do — pick up April? Leave before they remembered I was there? "Never mind," Stacy said, going to April. "It's just hair."

Darren laughed. "That's what I'm saying."

"Okay then." Stacy sat on the edge of the bed with April and it seemed like the fight was over. Darren looked at me and shrugged, then went into the bathroom to shower.

As soon as the door closed, Stacy muttered real low, "Fuck you, Darren."

I couldn't think of anything to say. Of all the ways I'd imagined Stacy and Darren and April and me as a family, I never pictured this.

I almost didn't go to work that night. Dealing with Tommy, seeing the booth where I'd crapped all over Lee's friendship, and facing customers all seemed like too much on top of the weirdness between Darren and Stacy. I wanted to walk over to Jason's, but I was afraid. I mean, what if Lee had told him about how I'd treated her? If he was forced to choose between her and me . . . well, I just wasn't ready to hear which one of us it would be. So when it was time for Stacy to leave for work, and she knocked twice on my door and said, "Let's go," I went.

She didn't talk on the ride over. Instead, she rifled through her CDs while attempting to drive, putting one after the other in the CD player, finding her favorite songs, and blasting them at full volume. I noticed also that she'd squeezed herself into her tightest jeans and left the dark makeup on.

"Did you and Darren, like, *talk*?" I asked between songs.

"About what?"

Okay, I thought, if she's going to play it that way then just forget it. In twenty-four hours she'd gone from wanting to take me to a bar to treating me like an annoying little kid. When we got to Picasso's, I got out without saying anything and slammed the door, trying not to think: What if *this* was the life in store when we moved out together? It couldn't be like that. It had to be okay; it was probably just Stacy's postpartum hormones making her act this way.

It was a busy night. The summer softball leagues had started up, and all these middle-aged guys trying to relive high school came in, their big bellies packed into dirty softball shirts, ordering pitchers of beer and basically acting like jackasses. We didn't work too bad together, actually, when it came down to crunch time. Tommy prepped the crusts and ran the oven, I took orders and did toppings, Michael handled everything else.

"Push the salad bar," he told us. "We're running low on pepperoni."

"I *think* they're gonna know the difference," Tommy said.

I took orders, saying, "The salad bar is only $2.99," about nine hundred times. "It's all you can eat."

Still, Michael had to run out at ten to buy more pepperoni and ground beef. The softball people started to clear out, and I bused their tables while Tommy cleaned up the pizza line.

That's when a parade of people from my worst nightmares walked through the door: Jake Millard, senior; Anthony Picollini, senior; Jolene Hancock, graduated; and her brother, Mike, senior. All of them had been at Terra Nova with Tommy. All of them were in his circle of friends.

Jolene was the first to spot me and start laughing. "No way! Deanna Lambert works here?" She called over to Tommy, "That must be convenient, huh?" Like I wasn't standing right there; like I was nobody.

"Hey, Lambert," Mike said, "just can't stay away from Tommy? I guess he's as good as he says he is."

Tommy came out from behind the counter, grinning. "They always come back for more."

I carried my trays of garbage into the back.

"Aw, don't be like that, Deanna," Jake called after me. "We all know Tommy's a shithead!"

They laughed. I leaned against the dishwasher, warm on my back, and closed my eyes.

This is my life, I thought. This is it. When I'm thirty-five years old picking up tampons and a loaf of bread at the store and I run into Jolene Hancock in the express line, she'll look at me and when she gets home she'll tell her husband, "I saw Deanna Lambert at the store. She's this girl I knew in high school. Kind of skanky. Slept with this gross junior when she was only thirteen."

I didn't know if I had any friends left. I didn't know if Darren and Stacy were going to make it. I didn't know if my dad would ever be able to look at me and not think of that night at Montara Beach.

"Are you okay? Deanna?" I opened my eyes. It was Michael, holding a giant bag of pepperoni. "Are you crying?"

"No," I said. "I don't know. Sorry."

He put the pepperoni down. "Do you want to talk?"

Michael was nice. Sincerely nice; the nicest person I'd met in a long time. I liked his face, strong and interesting, with deep lines and the kind of skin you get when you smoke for twenty years. He knew the deal. And he didn't judge me, at least I don't think he did. But I couldn't talk to him, or anyone. The words just weren't in me.

"I've got a headache is all," I said, busying myself with loading the dishwasher.

"It has been a long night. Tommy's friends just left," he said. "In case you were wondering."

I pulled the lever to close the dishwasher, and pushed the start button. The sound of water spraying against metal kept me from having to answer.

Stacy didn't show up after work. Michael waited with me for a while and had a smoke, but at quarter to twelve said, "Look, I've got a hot date with my dentist early tomorrow morning. Are you going to be all right? Do you want a ride?"

"It's okay," I said. "My brother's girlfriend works over at Safeway. She probably just got delayed or something."

"Come on, I'll give you a ride to Safeway then."

"It's okay, I'll walk. It's just, like, a block." I didn't bother explaining that maybe Stacy was mad at me and that's why she hadn't shown up.

Michael threw his cigarette butt down and twisted it under

his boot. "No, you're coming with me. I can just imagine explaining to your parents why I let you walk when they find your dead body in a ditch."

I followed him to his car and we drove over to Safeway. "There's her car," I said when I spotted the Nova. "Thanks."

"Okay, kid." He looked at me like he was going to say something else, something important, and all I could think was, *Please don't be nice to me right now. Don't be understanding, don't be deep.* He must have read my mind, because his face changed and he only said, "See you tomorrow."

I went into the store looking for Stacy and asked a girl at one of the registers where she was.

"Oh," she said. "She left early. Wasn't feeling well."

"But her car is in the lot."

"Really? That's weird. She left around nine thirty."

I walked back outside and sat on a bench under the lights. The only thing I could figure was that Stacy had gotten so sick that she couldn't drive, and Darren picked her up with my mom's car or something and they forgot about me. If she was that sick, it might explain why she'd been in such a weird mood. It pissed me off a little that they wouldn't think about how I'd just be left hanging in the middle of the night, but I didn't want to call Darren's cell and rock the boat. And I didn't want to call my parents, obviously.

The stupid SamTrans bus didn't run at night, so I started walking home, wishing I still smoked. A cigarette always felt a little like I had company, plus I figured I could use a lit cigarette as a weapon if someone tried to attack me.

Fog clung to me with the kind of damp cold that soaks through your clothes and skin and goes right to your bones. I tucked my hair under my jacket and walked different — with my hands in my pockets and my shoulders hunched over — like Darren had taught me, so that I'd look more like a guy in the dark. After I'd walked for about ten minutes, a car slowed down alongside me. I started walking faster and looking for houses that still had lights on in case I needed to run somewhere. The car stayed with me and then I heard that easy voice, "Hey, Dee Dee." I didn't stop. Tommy kept driving next to me, talking out of the open window.

"Dee Dee, come on. You need a ride? Hey I'm not going to jump you or anything. Unless you want me to. But seriously, get in the car, will you?"

I was cold and tired and had another fifteen minutes to go before home. Tommy was a lot of things I hated, but I knew it was true what he said, that he wouldn't do anything. That would screw up the image he had of himself as a stud that girls flocked to on their own, though I'd never personally seen that happen. I stopped, opened the car door, and jumped in while the car still moved along slowly.

"Stacy didn't show, huh?"

"Obviously."

"She always was kind of a flake." He never knew when to

shut up. "Hey, let's have a little smoke while we're at it." He pulled a joint out of his pocket and lit it while steering with his elbows. I shook my head when he held it out to me. "Oh yeah, you're a good girl now. I forgot."

Being in Tommy's car with the pot smoke and the damp night air triggered a rush of memories, stuff I hadn't thought about in a long time. Like our first "date," about a week after that day in the bathroom. Tommy showed up at our house one night, a rainy Tuesday, and asked for Darren. Darren had worked Tuesday nights for almost a year and Tommy knew it.

"He's not here," I'd said. I remember watching him, knowing he was there for *me*, not Darren, that it was a game we were playing.

"Oh." He gave me a little smile and his scar wrinkled up in a way that made my stomach jump, back then. He leaned in the doorway, in his black T-shirt and jeans jacket, like the house belonged to him and anything in it was his for the taking. "I just wanted to go for a drive, you know. I like driving in the rain." He looked over my shoulder. "Are your parents home?"

My mom was at work and my dad had gone to bed early after pulling a long shift at a temp job. It was after he'd been laid off from National Paper, but before the auto store, and it seemed like all he did was hunt for jobs or temp or sleep.

Tommy said, really cheerful-like, "Hey, I have an idea. You want to go for a drive with me? We could stop and get some ice cream, you know. I've got a craving for mint chocolate-chip ice cream."

"I don't know," I said, even though I did know. "I have homework."

"Do it later."

I grabbed my jacket and keys and walked out the door with him without even thinking about it, like part of me had been waiting for him to show up like that, with some lame excuse for going out, ever since that day in the bathroom.

We drove down the coast that night and parked in the lot at Montara Beach, where Tommy lit a joint. "You don't want any of this," he'd said. "You're too young and sweet."

"You have no idea what goes on in junior high, do you," I said, taking the joint from him. Still playing the game.

"It's been a while." He watched me take a hit. My friend at the time, Melony Fletcher, was sort of a pot head and I'd smoked a little with her. It wasn't my favorite thing in the world but I wanted to show Tommy I wasn't a kid.

"You have to *promise* not to tell your brother about this," Tommy said. "Promise?"

"It's none of his business. I have my own life."

We smoked and listened to the radio and then Tommy moved the bench seat back, put his long arm behind me, and said, "Come here."

It was like I was watching myself slide over toward him, watching myself let him pull me onto his lap while I laughed and laughed, goofy from the pot. It didn't seem so bad. I knew plenty of girls at school who had what they called boyfriends, but they didn't go out on dates. Their boyfriends were just guys they made out with after school while their parents were at work. Some of them were having sex—including Melony, with Mitch Benedict.

Tommy said, "I just want to look at your pretty face. Up close." His face was an inch from mine and I stopped laughing. "You're so pretty. You're prettier than any of the girls in high school. They all look so made up and used up and fake, not like you."

Not like me. Those words rang in my head, bouncing around with the pot and the dizziness of being alone with Tommy, in his car, a boy — a *man* — telling me I had something other girls didn't.

I touched his scar, something I'd wanted to do since I first saw him. It felt soft, like regular skin, not how I expected. He took my fingers and kissed them. "It's not cool," he said, "you know, kissing your friend's little sister."

"It's okay," I said. "Like I said, it's none of his business."

"I agree." But he still wouldn't kiss me; he just stared at me and squeezed my hip and smiled until finally I kissed him. He liked to remind me about that all during the next months when I would say we should stop doing what we were doing. "Hey," he'd say, "you started it, remember?"

So we made out that night and never did get ice cream, me trying to keep the game going because it was the only thing in my life that felt any good. After that, Tommy would pick me up from school sometimes and take me driving, or would show up on the nights Darren worked and it kept on like that for almost a year before anyone found out.

Later, after he told everyone about my dad finding us, Tommy didn't seem so cool and tough and smooth, he just seemed like a sleazy loser and I could see why girls in high school weren't interested in him. Even Melony, who had a key chain that said "99% Virgin," dropped me after it got around about Tommy. It took me awhile to figure that out, why *Melony* cared about reputation, until I started hearing the way Tommy had described the story to everyone. He made it into a joke. He made *me* into a joke.

But Lee was right. Tommy had something. And even when he was all gross from the pizza place and stoned and driving me home from Safeway after Stacy didn't show, there was a part of me that remembered how it felt when he chose *me:* that first time he told me I was pretty, that first time I kissed him. I remembered, too, how it felt when I finally realized it wasn't a game and it wasn't something I was watching on TV. It was something real happening between two real people. Me, *I* felt real; feeling real feelings, saying real words.

"House looks the same," Tommy said, pulling up to our curb. "Your old man still crazy?"

"He's not crazy."

"Okay, depressed or repressed or whatever." I got out of the car and slammed the door. He called through the window: "Aren't you going to thank me for the ride?"

"Thanks for the ride. Now leave."

"All right, all right. Jesus."

He drove away and I went into the house. The basement

light was on and it looked like Darren and Stacy were still up. When I got halfway down the stairs, Darren appeared at the bottom.

"Nice of you guys to finally show up," he said in a loud whisper. "I was about to take Mom's car to go out looking."

"What are you talking about? I waited around for forty-five minutes and no one ever showed!"

Darren motioned for me to come all the way downstairs and we went into the little bathroom, closing the door so we wouldn't wake April. "Stacy isn't with you?" he asked.

"No," I said, feeling something that scared me. "She's not here?"

"Shit," said Darren, running his hands through his short hair.

"The car is in the Safeway lot," I said. "They said she left early, at nine thirty."

"Well where is she, then?" Darren said. "Where is she?"

I pulled the comp book out from behind my bed and stared at a blank page for half an hour.

I didn't want to write about the girl on the waves anymore.

I was scared to write about anything else.

7.

Early the next morning, my mom drove Darren down to Safeway to pick up the Nova. Stacy had left a note in the car: "Don't worry about me. I'm sorry." Nothing about where she was or why she left or if she was coming back. Mom and Darren called in sick to work, but Dad said he couldn't afford to miss a day just to go chasing after Stacy.

"She'll be back," he said. "She just wants the attention."

Darren didn't respond, but I saw his hand clench around April's bottle.

"What kind of a mother leaves her baby?" Dad continued, looking around the kitchen for some kind of support.

"Don't want to hear it, Dad," Darren said.

For once, Dad actually shut up about Stacy and left Darren

alone. He didn't exactly offer to help or say anything to make it better, but at least he stopped talking and left for work.

Mom poured a cup of coffee for Darren, who sat at the table with April cradled in his arms. "Let's just stay by the phone," Mom said. "I bet we'll hear from her any minute." She rested her hand on Darren's head for a second in a way I hadn't seen her do for a long time. "Stacy probably just needed to get away for a little bit."

As usual, Mom refused to see the reality of the situation, choosing instead to believe that everything would eventually work itself out by some sort of magic.

"Mom," Darren said quietly, "if she needed to get away all she had to do was tell me. She knows that."

"Well. You never know. Hormones can make a young mother crazy . . ."

Darren got up with April and left the kitchen. I followed him into my room. "What are you going to do?" I asked. He put April on my bed on her stomach and shoved his hands way down into his pockets, eyes on the floor.

"I don't know." His voice broke and his shoulders started shaking and then he just stood there in the middle of my room, crying but trying not to make too much noise, my big brother who could deal with anything. April stopped her own sounds and lifted her little head as best she could to look at Darren. Neither of us had ever seen him cry before. He covered his face with both his hands. "I'm sorry."

If I were a different kind of sister, a better kind, I would have hugged him and told him everything would be okay. Maybe if we were out of my parents' house, in our own place, we could be that kind of family. But here, we were the same old Lamberts we'd always been. And besides, for all I knew, nothing would ever be okay again.

Darren made some calls to Stacy's family but no one had heard from her, and they didn't seem to care, which was typical. They were almost as screwed up as we were. Stacy's mom didn't want to have anything to do with April because she thought April never should have been born.

Sometimes I wonder, you know, what's wrong with some families. Like mine, and like Stacy's. I look at people like Lee, with her mom and stepdad so nice, and I know that's how a family should be, and I realize how fucked up it is to not be talking to each other and to be blaming each other and not wanting to know anything about your own grandkid. I'm sorry, but it's just fucked up.

Used to be I'd think about that stuff and just go, okay, no big deal, it will be different with me and Stacy and Darren. We'll *make* it different. But with Stacy leaving the way she did, I started to think the truth was that we didn't know how. We didn't know how any better than Mom and Dad did.

Darren didn't want to call the police; he worried they might end up taking April away. So he left April with me and went driving around to some of his and Stacy's favorite places in the city and around Pacifica.

I called Jason. I thought maybe if I had a reason to talk to him, with big news like Stacy disappearing, he'd kind of have to keep listening even if Lee had already told him about our fight.

"There you are," he said when he answered the phone. "I thought you died or something."

I smiled, relieved. He didn't hate me; not yet, anyway. "It's only been a couple of days."

"Well I've been bored. Let's do something."

It's funny how just a couple of words from him could make me feel a million times better. I almost didn't want to spoil the good feeling by talking about Stacy, but I needed someone outside of our house to know so that it wouldn't be something I had to carry around on my own.

"Holy shit," he said after I told him, "she seems like such a good mom."

"She is."

"She'll come back," he said. "I bet she'll be back tonight." We were quiet on the phone for a minute. I pictured him: breathing, his dark hair hanging over his eyes; probably slumped into the old armchair he'd moved into his room in eighth grade. Maybe scratching his stomach. "Hello?"

"Yeah, I'm here. Let's go out to Serramonte or something. Tomorrow?"

We made our plans, me feeling like I'd been given a little

gift — at least another week before Jason heard Lee's side of the story. When I got off the phone, April started fussing. I picked her up and walked around the house with her over my shoulder, but that only made her cry more and I couldn't get her to stop. Her crying sounded more scared than tired or hungry. It was like she'd figured out Stacy was gone, and not just to work. I went into the kitchen to make a bottle anyway, not sure what else to do.

Dad was sitting at the kitchen table; I sucked in a lungful of air in surprise, loud, which made April cry even harder. Dad seemed startled, too. When I caught my breath, I said, "I thought you went to work."

He kept his eyes on his National Paper coffee cup. "I did. When I got there I told them I had a family emergency and came home."

"Oh." I shifted April around and tried to work on her bottle with one hand, holding her close to me with the other. The top of the bottle fell to the floor when I tried to screw it on, and when I picked up the top, I dropped the bottom part and formula spilled all over the floor. "Shit."

Whatever good feeling I'd gotten from talking to Jason was already gone, and now I felt myself start to lose it. What if Stacy never came back? I couldn't picture me and Darren doing all this stuff for April for a couple of days, never mind the rest of our lives.

Dad picked the bottle up off the floor and set it on the counter. I figured he'd lecture me about my mouth and how I shouldn't swear in front of April, or about how this was the way it would be now that Stacy had deserted us so I'd better get used to it. Instead, he reached out his arms. "Here. Let me take her while you fix the bottle."

April, still crying, turned her head at the sound of his voice. He'd only held her once as far as I knew, right when she got back from the hospital. Usually he left the room when she cried. "That's okay," I said. "I can do it."

"I'm sure you can. But I do know how to hold a baby. I had two of my own." April's crying had reached that red-faced, squinty-eyed scary stage and now I had to sterilize the bottle and start all over. So I handed her over to Dad.

When he took her, he had to stand closer to me than he had for a long time. I could feel the warmth of him and the aftershave he'd used since I was a kid, just this cheap stuff you can get at Safeway. I got this strong feeling of missing him, like he was someone who I loved who had died and gone away, someone who was mostly a memory. I wanted to grab him and say okay, I was sorry about Tommy, it was just a stupid mistake and I knew I'd hurt him and I wished I hadn't. Because I did love him. I did.

But then I remembered that night, and the way he looked at me like he didn't know me, and I'd cried in the car all the way home and I *did* say that I was sorry, over and over again. Then I said it about fifty more times in the days after that, and he never did more than shake his head or leave the room.

And I said I was sorry again after he got the job at the auto parts store and overheard his twenty-year-old manager telling a sixteen-year-old employee one of the versions of me, a variation of the nympho version: *Yeah, that's Deanna Lambert's dad, you know, the one who got in a fight with Tommy Webber because he found them, right? Him and Deanna, that skanky eighth grader, going at it and she was loving it, you know, and then her dad shows up, and that's him, working in the parts department.*

He, my father, repeated the whole thing to me and Mom, his voice loud there in the kitchen and I said I was sorry, *again,* and wanted to tell him that's not how it happened, not what I was like at all. But why should I have to defend myself, convince my own father, my dad who knew me forever, that I wasn't like that? And wouldn't any father, *any* father, have gone up to those guys at the auto shop, those guys who were half his age, and made a declaration for me: *Hey, that's my daughter you're talking about. My daughter.* And come home and not said anything about it, not humiliated me all over again.

That's what I figured out that day while he yelled at me. That as much as I'd let him down, he'd let me down, too, and he was the one who should know better. He was the dad. He was *my* dad. That's when I had to make myself stop loving him. I had to stop remembering the way he used to be, the way we used to be, because if I kept thinking about the old dad every time I looked at him, it would never stop hurting.

And that's why I couldn't touch him now and try I'm sorry one more time. I didn't have it in me to be turned away again.

Dad had April, patting her on the back, gently bouncing her

up and down. He headed for the kitchen door and I blurted, "Where are you going?"

"Just down the hall," he said. "If that's all right."

I turned to run the hot water for sterilizing the bottle. Dad talked to April in the hall, not like baby talk, but in his normal voice. "Deanna's fixing you up a bottle now, okay? She's fixing it right up." I tilted my head toward the sound of my name, the way April had turned to his voice earlier. He hadn't said my name in forever. At least, not that I'd heard. I'd been "you" and "she" for a long time. He kept talking about other stuff, how Darren would be home soon and Mom's car needed a new windshield. After a minute, April's crying turned into little sobs and whimpers, and by the time I was done with her bottle she wasn't crying at all.

Dad stood in the doorway. "I used to do that with you," he said. "I'd walk up and down the hall and tell you about my day and anything else I could think to talk about."

I thought then, *right* then, that something still could have happened. The last three years could be a bad memory. I could say, *Dad, let's just try,* and he could look at April in his arms and nod quietly, and everything could be different, couldn't it?

The moment went by, and Darren walked in and asked, "What's going on?" He looked at April, resting her head on Dad's shoulder, holding his shirt collar in her little hand.

"I'm just about to give her a bottle," I said, concentrating on folding and refolding the dish towel. "She wouldn't stop crying after you left."

"I think she's ready for a nap," Dad said. He handed April over to Darren and left the room, his back straight and stiff. We watched him go without saying anything, then I threw the dish towel on the counter and put the bottle in the fridge. How come he could be like that with April all of a sudden? So nice, so . . . *fatherly*. Maybe it meant he could be like that with me if he tried, if he wanted to. Only I guess he didn't want to.

"What was that all about?" Darren asked.

I shrugged. "He picked her up, she stopped crying."

He leaned against the counter, holding April to his chest. He looked tired; big circles under his eyes, lips tight. "Remember last summer? When all we did was drive around looking for parties?"

Used to be he would get home from work and then me and him would pick up Stacy and sometimes Jason, then get something cheap to eat. If we had any money we'd go to a movie. Otherwise we'd drive around the valley or into the city and try to find a party or at least somewhere to walk around for a couple of hours. That was after Tommy, when Darren liked to keep me with him so that he knew where I was, and before Stacy found out she was pregnant, before I met Lee. To be honest, I couldn't really remember any of the parties or anything specific we did that I'd call a good time.

"Yeah," I said, "but mostly we were just trying to get out of the house. I mean, did we actually have any fun?"

"I don't know." Darren rubbed the fuzz on April's head and yawned. "But I'd like the chance to do it again right about now."

We were quiet, both staring at the kitchen floor, the ugly yellow linoleum that had been there since Mom and Dad bought the house, in hideous contrast to the pink walls. "Where do you think she is?" I asked. "Where could she have gone without the car?"

"She could be anywhere. She could be at someone's house in Pacifica. Maybe she hitched, maybe she met a guy, I don't know." He sounded angry now, not scared anymore.

"Met a *guy*?" I asked. "Like, when? In between changing diapers and doing laundry and working?"

"I know, I know. She probably didn't meet a guy."

I thought hard about what I said next. I didn't want to blame Darren or make him feel bad or anything like that, but if he was as clueless as he seemed I thought maybe it would help. "She wanted you to notice, Darren. To notice how amazing and different and mysterious she looked."

"What are you talking about?"

"Her hair, you know, how she dyed her hair."

He stared. "She's mad about her *hair*?"

"No, jackass." I should have kept my mouth shut if I couldn't explain it. "It's just . . . you kind of acted like it was cute, like it was nothing."

Darren got louder. "Again I ask: She's mad about her *hair*?"

"Forget it, never mind. She's not mad about her hair."

"No, explain it to me. You obviously have some great insight into this whole situation."

April started to cry again. "It's like what she said when she looked in the mirror," I said. "She could have been anyone, you know?"

"No, I don't know."

I sighed and got the bottle back out of the fridge, warmed it in the microwave for a few seconds, and handed it to Darren. He tested it and gave it to April. "Like, what if she hadn't had April? She might be in college or backpacking across Europe or something. She looked like that kind of girl."

Darren was silent for a minute, watching April suck on her bottle. "And that's a reason to leave? Because I didn't get all that from a dye job?" He looked at me. "What if she doesn't come back?"

"She has to."

Later, I went down to the basement to see if Darren had heard anything. He sat on the edge of the bed, channel surfing, while April slept in her car seat on the floor. Not exactly a picture for the family photo album I kept in my head.

"Do you want me to bring you a pizza tonight or anything?" I asked.

"Yeah, okay. Thanks." He didn't take his eyes off the TV even though it was just a commercial. I sat next to him and flipped through one of Stacy's magazines; April woke up and started to cry.

"Come on," Darren said, dropping the remote, "nap time ain't over. You can do better than that." He picked her up and took her over to the crib. She quieted down after a couple of minutes of him standing over her and talking soft, with no idea he was doing the exact same thing Dad had done earlier.

Then he was quiet and froze, staring at the lighthouse poster over the crib.

"Hellooo," I said.

He turned around and looked at me funny. "Come here."

I did. "Yeah?"

"Look." He pointed to the print at the bottom of the poster, which read, *Pigeon Point Light Station State Historic Park.*

"So?"

"That's where I took her for her birthday last year. It's in Pescadero."

For a second I wondered if Darren was having some kind of breakdown or going into shock or something. "Like I said: so?"

"I don't know. You know how she is about lighthouses. And there's a youth hostel there," he said. "It's really cheap . . ."

It seemed like a long shot to me, but he sounded so hopeful and anyway, he knew her better than I did. "Is there a phone number?"

"I don't want to call. If she's there, I don't want her to know I'm coming."

After the whole scene in the kitchen with my dad — the way he held April, the way he almost really looked at me — I was an easy target for getting pulled into Darren's hopefulness. "We could leave first thing tomorrow," I said. "You can pack while I'm at work."

"I'm going tonight," Darren said. He got a duffle bag out of the closet and started throwing stuff into it while I watched, already knowing the truth of what was about to happen.

"But I have to work," I said. "Can't you wait?"

He looked at me and shook his head.

"I'll call work and tell them I can't come in tonight."

"You're not coming with me."

I couldn't listen to what he was saying. I couldn't let him say what I knew he was going to say next, or soon, or eventually. "You need someone to help you with April," I said, my voice starting to wobble.

"Not really."

There's this picture of Darren and Stacy, a snapshot I took a few days before April was born. They kept it on their nightstand in a purple plastic frame I'd picked up at Walgreens. I concentrated on it, ignoring what Darren had said. "You think you're going to drive two hours with April screaming her head off after you haven't slept for, like, twenty-four hours?"

"Don't be such a drama queen," he said. "I deal with April all the time. Anyway, she likes riding in the car."

My eyes fixed on the picture: Stacy in Darren's lap with her arm around his neck, Darren's hand on her big belly. Anyone could see it. They were already a family. Darren and Stacy and

April, they didn't need me to complete them. Them: a family. Me: always the extra, unnecessary, undeclared nobody.

Maybe I knew it all along; maybe that's why I never actually talked to them about it, my plan for all of us living together.

"Fine," I said. "Go without me."

"Come on, Deanna. Don't be like that."

"You're not even packing the right stuff for April. She needs, like, twice as many diapers as that."

He stopped packing and came toward me. "Deanna . . ." His voice was big brotherly, like, *Okay, I gotta be nice to my sister or she's going to start crying and then I'll be stuck here dealing with it.*

"Don't," I said, backing up. The room blurred. "Forget it, it's okay. Just go. I don't care."

"Yes, you do. Look, you know we're moving out as soon as we can. You and me can't do everything together." I wished he would stop talking; I wished I'd never come downstairs. "This," he said, "*this* is something I definitely have to do alone."

"I know." I crossed the room and started folding the endless pile of laundry on the bed. I couldn't cry. I wouldn't.

"I mean, we might as well get used to it, you know?"

I tried, I did, to keep from saying anything else, but I was outside of it now, watching myself turn into a big baby right in front of him, all the time thinking I should just shut up. "Why not?" I asked, turning toward him.

"Why not what?"

"Why couldn't I live with you guys?"

There, I thought. I said it. I wouldn't pretend anymore that it wasn't what I wanted, that it made no difference to me.

He rubbed his hands over his face. "Shit. Deanna, don't do this right now, okay?"

"I could watch April in the afternoons," I said, pleading. "And clean the house and help with the rent and everything."

Then he laughed. He actually laughed and shook his head.

"It's not a joke!"

April whimpered.

Darren stopped. "I know. But have you been paying attention? Stacy and I have to get our shit together, like, *now*. I mean, look at us! We have the kid and maybe that wasn't the smartest thing we ever did, but there she is. We live in the basement of our extremely fucked-up parents." He went back to his packing. "It's not a good start, Deanna, is what I'm saying."

"But you guys manage!" My voice dissolved into the tears I'd been determined not to cry. "I could *help*. I could. I could help."

"We *manage*? Stacy's gone! Doesn't that tell you anything?"

"Don't yell at me!"

"I'm . . ." He lowered his voice. "I'm not. Deanna, me and Stacy have to do more than manage. Mom and Dad? They manage. April deserves better than that." He zipped the duffle and put on his jacket. "So do I."

"And *I* deserve to stay here and keep eating shit?"

"No," he said, sighing. "But you're gonna have to find your own way out."

I dropped the laundry I'd been holding onto: a tiny T-shirt of April's, a pair of Stacy's socks.

I turned around.

I walked up the stairs.

I did not look back.

7A.

I, Deanna Lambert, belong to no one, and no one belongs to me.

I don't know what to do.

78.

Darren left around four. He knocked on my door and asked, through the wall, if I wanted him to drop me off at work on his way down the coast, but I pretended not to hear. When he was gone I went to the kitchen and made myself some ramen. Mom came back from running errands while I ate, dragging into the kitchen looking like she could be my grandma instead of my mom, all gray roots and droopy eyelids.

"There's leftover pot roast," she said, setting her big purse on the table. She went straight to the fridge and started pulling stuff out. The cold smell of old but not quite spoiled food wafted across the room. "Or I could make you a sandwich. There's also spaghetti from Wednesday night."

"This is what I want."

"Are you sure? How about a can of soup? Can I heat you up a can of soup?"

"This *is* soup." She still had her head in the fridge, her back to me. "God, Mom, can't you stop for one second?"

That got her to turn around, her face drawn, and all of her small somehow. Her hands were on her hips in that way she used to do when Darren or I were in trouble and she'd say, *Deanna Louise, I told you not to touch that* or *Darren Christopher, leave your sister alone!* But this time she let her hands drop without scolding me and turned to the counter. "Well, I'm going to make myself a pot roast sandwich. With lots of onion. I've been thinking about it all day."

I rinsed out my bowl and watched Mom make her sandwich. "I don't guess we heard anything from Stacy?" she asked.

"No. But . . ." I had a hard time even saying his name. "Darren had an idea where she might be. He just left with April."

"Oh!" Mom actually smiled. "Well, that is good news. Hopefully she'll be back in her own bed tonight." Like it was that easy. Like Stacy could just come back and everything would be like nothing had ever happened, the same way Mom wanted it to be between me and Dad.

"I have to go to work," I said.

She did stop, then, and look at me, a cloud of concern passing over her already-worn face. "Honey? Have you been crying?"

I shook my head.

She stepped toward me, put her hand on my cheek.

I pulled away.

Her hand withdrew, left to hang by her side. "Well. Do you want a ride to work?"

I shook my head again, got my stuff, and left.

8.

Work was typical: Tommy acting like an asshat, customers confused by the handwritten menu, the salad bar giving off its usual stink. About ten minutes before closing, Michael got a call. His niece was stranded at the Colma BART station and he had to give her a ride home.

"Can you two close up without me?"

"Sure," Tommy said, popping a couple of olives into his mouth. "It's not rocket science."

"Lucky for you," Michael said.

On his way out, he asked me if I'd be all right there alone with Tommy. "You can leave now if you want," he said. It was nice, you know, the way Michael looked out for me that way. Too bad I didn't know him when I was thirteen.

"I'll stay," I said. "It's not like there's anything or anyone waiting for me at home." Michael gave me a look, and I cringed at the self-pity in my voice. I didn't want to turn into one of those *look-at-me-my-life-is-so-hard* people. "Go," I said, trying to sound cheerful. "We got it covered."

The second Michael was out the door, Tommy turned up the jukebox, punching up his usual playlist of cheesy '80s rock. I bleached the cutting boards while Tommy cleaned the bathrooms, sometimes stopping to play air guitar on the mop.

"Hey, Dee Dee," he called from the women's room, "gimme your friend's phone number."

"Stop calling me that. I mean it." I plunged my gloved hands into the bucket of bleach water, heat burning through the green latex. "And if you mean Lee, she's taken."

He stood in the bathroom doorway with the mop in his hands, the corners of his mouth curled up into a smile, that smile that pissed me off and sped up my heart all at once. "Jealous, huh? Don't want to give up the digits?"

I walked away from him and into the back to dump the bucket. He followed me. "Can't you ever just be *nice* to me?" I asked, rinsing the stainless-steel sink. "You used to be so *nice* sometimes." It was true. There were times he would listen to me talk about school, chiming in sometimes to say this or that teacher was a prick, laughing when I told him about something funny that had happened. I always liked that part of it, how he would listen and just go with it, not like a big brother or a parent, and not like a possessive boyfriend who wanted to know about every guy who talked to me in school. I'd just relive the day with him while he drove, and he'd listen.

Times like that, he'd been my friend. I hadn't thought the words "friend" and "Tommy" together for a long time, maybe ever. It now brought on a whole new wave of hurt at the way he'd treated me.

He stood by me at the sink, leaning on the mop. "I'm nice. I can be nice. Like for instance, I know you and your friend had a fight the other night, right? Tell me what happened. I'll listen. Nice."

I shook my head. "None of your business."

"Okay, fine," he said, wringing the mop out and hanging it on the wall with the broom and dustpan and other cleaning stuff. "How about this: I'll give you a ride home. That's how nice I am."

"I'd rather walk."

He laughed. "See, you don't *want* me to be nice." He untied his apron. "I'm just bad old Tommy, the one who ruined your life, right? Whatever works for you."

We finished cleaning up, took the garbage out, and locked the door. Tommy lit a cigarette, the flame of the lighter illuminating his face. A shadow flickered across the scar on his left cheek.

I remembered touching that scar our first night together.

At least back then, I belonged to someone. Tommy had chosen me, and whatever it really was, the two of us were *something*, something that we weren't without each other.

It was cold out and foggy and no one would be coming to get me. Darren had made his choice, and it didn't include me. Jason had Lee. Mom and Dad . . . well, the whole idea of parents seemed like a part of ancient history.

Tommy didn't scare me; I knew what he was all about.

"Yeah, okay," I said. "I'll take a ride home."

He looked at me sideways, like to see if I was serious. He shivered a little in the fog and for once seemed to have run out of smart-ass remarks. "Come on."

We walked to his car. He opened the passenger door for me. I slid into the bench seat and as he closed the door behind me with a thunk, I knew what was going to happen next.

He got in, fired up the engine. He pulled out of the space and drove slowly to the parking lot exit and stopped. A right turn would take us to my house, where my parents were probably asleep and Darren and April were gone and I would lie alone in my room, awake in the dark, wondering what would happen to me. A left turn would take us toward Highway 1, and the old Chart House parking lot, a warm car on a cold night, me knowing exactly what to expect.

Tommy put on the left blinker. I didn't say anything.

I was never going to find a guy like Jason for myself. I knew it. I would never be that person, the one who made her parents proud and was there when her friends really needed her. I would never be part of Darren and Stacy's family, not the way I'd pictured.

Tommy turned left and pulled out onto the highway.

I rolled down my window a little. The fog was so thick that I couldn't see even the road in front of us, never mind the dark of the ocean. I could smell it, though, the wet salt of it, as Tommy drove slow, the headlight beams bouncing off the wall of fog. He pulled into the lot and when he killed the lights, the ice plant–covered bluff was still there the way it had always been, the way it had been the night my dad followed us.

"You want to fire one up?" Tommy asked, digging in his pocket for a joint.

"No, thanks." Beyond the bluff was more fog, and beneath that the beach, and then the ocean and then nothing past that but horizon, I knew. "I'll take a cigarette, though," I said.

Darren would kill me if he knew, after how he'd helped me quit, but it was all part of the ritual that was Tommy and me. I knew it just like I knew the ocean was there even though I couldn't see it. He handed me a smoke and his lighter. I put the cigarette between my lips and flicked the lighter a couple of times before it caught, then inhaled deeply, like I used to. It made me cough; Tommy laughed. When I could talk, I just said, "Shit," and put the cigarette out after taking one more little puff.

Tommy put the lighter back in his pocket and messed with the car radio for a few seconds — more ritual — before turning it off and saying, "Don't want to drain the battery."

"Right."

Next should have been him reaching over and rubbing my shoulder while I talked and finished my cigarette, but since I'd already put it out we were off the playbook now. I could have told him I wanted to go home; he would have taken me. There was one other car in the lot, way over in the south corner. I wondered if the people in it were like me and Tommy, or more like Jason and Lee. Or maybe there was just one person, alone, someone else who didn't want to go home.

Tommy drummed his hands on the steering wheel. "Soooo . . ." He tried to give me his cocky grin but it only looked afraid. I slid over to him on the bench seat of the car and he kissed me. It was like a first kiss, shy and short, not a kiss I expected from someone I'd made out with a hundred times before.

We kissed some more and it didn't take long for that shyness to wear off, and soon we were back to where we'd left off all those years ago and I let his hands go wherever. I don't remember now how it felt. I wanted it to feel good. I wanted it to feel something. I wanted to remember what it had been like when I was thirteen, if I could figure out why I'd gone along with Tommy and everything he said and did. Was it only because he happened to be the one who came along when he did? Could it have been anyone? Or was there something about him, Tommy Webber, that I liked and cared about? There in the Buick with the fog all around us, I tried to connect with my thirteen-year-old self, remember what she felt like, what she wanted.

We kept making out and Tommy took my Picasso's shirt off. We both smelled like pizza. He reached down the side of the bench seat and slid it back, then there was the old thing — the soft but steady pressure on my shoulder with one hand, the other gently pulling on my hair. The first time he did that I was confused, not sure what he wanted. But I wasn't completely stupid and I'd heard about it from Melony, and, I mean, I guess it's just human instinct to sort of figure it out. I remember that first time I didn't want to do it, really, I just wanted to keep kissing and stuff like we had been. But I was stoned and it seemed like a reasonable alternative to going all the way and I didn't want him to get mad at me. I didn't want it all to stop.

"Come on, Dee Dee," he said now.

I pushed against his hand and sat up. "Can't you just . . ." I didn't know what I wanted to say. "I don't want to right now."

"Yeah, you do. Come on. Please? You used to love doing that." It was both sad and funny, you know, how two people's memory of the same thing could be so different. And that was the whole problem, really, that this thing had happened between us, and to Tommy it was one thing and to me it was something else, and once my dad got involved it became something else again. Three people at the scene of the crime, each with a different story. Add onto that the whole jury known as Terra Nova High School and who knew anymore what had really happened?

I grabbed my shirt and got out of the car. I stood outside in the fog, in my bra, turning my shirt right-side-out. Someone in the other car rolled down their window and I heard a girl yell, "Are you okay?"

"Yeah, no problem," I called across the lot. I put my shirt

back on, and Tommy got out on his side, looking at me across the shiny top of the car.

"What's wrong?"

"I didn't used to love doing that," I said.

"Okay." He smiled. "But *I* liked it when you did that, and I know I made you feel good, too. I *know* that. I always gave as good as I got."

"I didn't say it didn't feel good . . ." They never tell you this part in sex ed, how to talk about what you did and why you did it and what you thought about it, before, during, and after.

"Then what are you talking about?" He folded his arms on the roof of the car and leaned on them. "What's the problem?"

"The problem," I started. "Just . . . the whole thing . . ." Then I was crying and couldn't stop. Twice in one day with the crying. Tommy's smirk went away and he came over to my side of the car. This would be where a regular guy, an ex who cared about you, would, like, give you a hug or something, right? Tommy could only stare and look like he wanted to be anywhere else.

"What? What did I do?"

"God, Tommy! I was thirteen!" He watched me cry some more. "Can't you say anything?" I asked. "I'd never even gone on a date. I still haven't."

"And that's my fault?"

"You were seventeen. Supposedly Darren's best friend." I wiped my arm across my face, trying to calm down. "You know I could have pressed charges? There are laws."

"But you didn't."

"I *know*. That's not . . . What if you had a little sister," I said, "and Darren did all that shit to her you did to me?"

" 'Did' you to you? What's that supposed to mean?" He seemed sincerely confused. "Are you saying I, like, *raped* you? Because if you're saying that . . ."

"No. No, I — you never even took me out. We never went to a movie. We never just hung out and watched TV." *We never held hands, we never went for a walk, we never went out for anything to eat.* The longer the list got in my head, the more pathetic I felt. The more I felt hurt, the more I felt angry, the more I felt everything. "What *was* I to you, Tommy? What did you think of me?"

"What did I *think* of you? I liked you, didn't I? I thought you were cute. I thought you were a turn-on."

"You thought I was an easy target, is what you thought. Right?"

"No, I . . ." He shrugged. "What do you want me to say?"

A wind kicked up off the ocean and everything moved, the trees and power lines and dune grass. The smell of salt and seaweed washed over us. That and the sound of the waves down on the beach and a car going by on the highway took me right back, right back to that year of being with Tommy a couple of times a week and then going home, Mom at work and Dad watching TV or looking at job ads in the paper or talking to his caseworker at the unemployment office, yelling at her, telling her how he'd been with National Paper nineteen years and they owed him, goddamnit, they *owed* him something. Or he'd be in his bed, asleep or just staring at the ceiling, and the house was quiet, quiet and angry, and I'd go straight to my room and tell myself that this was all temporary and pretty soon he'd get a job and Mom would be home more and someone would ask me where I'd been.

I looked at Tommy, his lean body and the hard, small muscles in his arms, the scar on his cheek, and okay, he'd meant something to me. When we were starting out, the way he wanted me and the way he listened to me, and what I'd given him, what we'd given each other, it *meant* something.

"Why'd you tell everyone, Tommy? You made it all into a big joke, just a big fucking funny story," I said. "Like none of it mattered."

He turned away from me, toward the beach.

I wiped my nose again. "It never should have been like that."

He went around to his side of the car and got in. I walked through the parking lot to get the rest of the tears out, exhausted and a little relieved. It felt like I'd been waiting to say that stuff to Tommy my whole life. He started the car and backed up like he was going to drive away, but then pulled to where I stood. "You getting in?"

The ride felt fast and familiar, like the times he'd be hurrying to get me home, the windows down to get the smell of pot out of the car.

When we got close to my house, a raccoon waddled out in front of the car. We both swore and Tommy put on the brakes.

The raccoon looked at us over its shoulder and lumbered off into someone's yard. Tommy drove slow the rest of the way.

And then there was the house: the peeling paint, the overgrown lawn, the abandoned flowerpots. The doorway Tommy had first leaned into, plucking me out of my old life and driving me into a new one. I ran my hand over the car door handle. I'd never really left that life; I could see that now. It had only been on pause. This, though, was an ending. Tommy wasn't for me. Okay, it was nice that he still wanted me, that I could still have that effect on him. But he wasn't exactly choosy.

I opened the car door.

Tommy stopped me, saying, "Deanna? If I really did all that . . . I mean, I know I did, but if all that was true about how you felt and everything . . . and, you know, how I talked about it, I'm sorry." He stared straight ahead, running his hands around the steering wheel.

"Me, too."

9.

I woke up to an empty house, which normally I wouldn't mind. Normally, that would be my preferred method of entry into any given day.

But nothing was normal.

Tommy is over.
I don't feel different.
Because: now what?
My life is a question mark.

I stared at the page. Maybe I should go back to the girl on the waves. At least I had some control over *her* life. If I could have taken a deep breath, thrown back the covers, and said,

"Today I'm starting over," maybe then things could be different. Like in a musical: la la la, I'll never be the same again, whatever. But when *I* took a deep breath and threw back the covers, I was still me.

The only good thing about the day ahead was Jason. We were supposed to go to the mall, like normal teenagers on summer vacation. I knew how to be a normal teenager: You make sarcastic comments, you act goofy and annoying. You buy stuff. You eat.

The phone rang; I let it ring a bunch of times before thinking it might be Darren. I got up and ran to answer it. It was my mom.

"I thought maybe you'd heard something," she said.

"No."

"Did you make it home from work all right?"

"Yeah." At first I thought, *No thanks to you, Mom,* then I remembered her hand on my face there in the kitchen, the look in her eyes. *Have you been crying?* She'd offered me something, at least.

"I might work some overtime tonight," she said.

"Aren't they cutting hours?"

"Well, a lot of people quit over that and now they're in a jam." She lowered her voice. "Typical corporate screwup, right? If you want to throw dinner together for your father, I think we have all the ingredients for tuna casserole . . ."

"I have to work tonight."

"Again? Well, I'll see you when I see you, huh?"

I pressed the phone to my cheek, imagining her hand there again. "Yeah, Mom. Okay."

After hanging up, I got my morning can of root beer from the fridge and stepped into the backyard. It was hot out already, no sign of the fog from the night before. I should have stayed outside and let the sun and warmth soak into my skin and my mind, but instead I went back in and flopped onto the couch with the TV remote. I surfed through the talk shows and pictured my dad on the screen. *Today's topic: My Daughter Is a Slut.* Tommy could go on, too, and tell the story to an international audience. Then maybe they'd get in a fight and some skinhead would break a chair over Tommy's head or give my dad a bloody nose.

No, I thought, *that's over.*

The front door opened and I jumped up, startled and ready to run. A redheaded woman was in my living room. When my brain caught up with my eyes, I realized it was Stacy.

"Hey," she said quietly. "I figured everyone would be at work. Except you. I knew you'd probably be home." She stood just inside the door, wearing the clothes she'd left in. "Can I come in?"

"Yeah." I stared, still startled by her dark hair. "Is Darren with you?"

Stacy frowned. "No. Isn't he at work?"

"He went looking for you. At that place in Pescadero, you know, the youth hostel?"

"What youth hostel?"

"The lighthouse," I said, getting impatient. "The one you stayed at that time? The poster is over April's crib?"

"Oh." She stepped into the room little by little, still looking like a guest or a stranger. "Why there?"

"He thought it was . . . never mind. Where *were* you?"

She hesitated, switching her purse from right shoulder to left. "At Kim's. Remember Corvette Kim?"

"Yeaahhh," I said slowly. "I didn't know you guys were still friends."

"She came to Safeway for a case of beer." Stacy touched her hair, like she was feeling for the color. "There was a party. She invited me. I went."

"You went to a *party*?"

"It's not like it sounds."

"For two days?"

She studied the floor. "I'm back now, okay?"

"You could have at least called." I thought about how she looked that night in the bathroom mirror, her hair wet and dark and no makeup on her face. Like she belonged somewhere else, not in a shitty basement with this screwed-up family. Now she was tired and sorry and I knew she was going to catch enough hell from Darren, not to mention my dad, so I left her alone. "April's with Darren," I said.

She nodded. "I'm gonna go downstairs."

When I heard the basement door close, I considered my options: call Darren or not call Darren. Calling to let him know Stacy was home could be, like, a peace offering. Something to let him know it was okay, I understood why he had to do what he did. Not calling him would be the opposite, maybe. The thing was that I didn't know if I was ready to have it either way.

I started out of the living room, away from the phone, then thought about April. I went back and called Darren's cell.

"She's here," I said.

"What?"

"Stacy's here." I knew he'd find out anyway, so I spilled it: "She was at Corvette Kim's." I could hear the sound of cars on the highway. "You want to talk to her?"

"No. Tell her to get out of my house."

"Darren."

"Tell her."

"I'm not going to tell her that," I said. "Just come home. And hurry up. I don't want Dad to get here first."

I hung up and immediately called Jason to remind him we were going to Serramonte. Given everything that was about to go down, it seemed stupid to stay around the house any longer than I had to.

"Dude," Jason said when he answered the phone, "I just woke up."

"Be at the bus stop in half an hour."

Jason came running down the hill just as the bus pulled up. He grinned as we climbed on board. "I got eighteen more minutes of sleep after you called," he said.

"You must be proud."

There were only three other passengers so we took the big seat across the back; me in one corner and him in the middle. Even with the space between us I could smell the clean scent of him, fresh out of the shower. His damp hair curled around the base of his neck in a way that made me want to touch it. I told myself to stop thinking like that — stop thinking about how Lee was out of town and how I'd known Jason longer, stop thinking about how Jason wanted to sleep with her and she probably wouldn't. I reminded myself that I was the New Deanna. I'd dealt with Tommy. Things had changed.

"It's so freakin' hot," Jason said. There was no sign — nothing in his voice or the way he looked at me — that Lee had said anything about our fight.

"I know," I said. "Which is why today is all about an air-conditioned mall." The bus rolled out of Pacifica and past the ugly rows of pastel stucco houses in Daly City. "So Stacy showed up today," I said.

"Told you she would."

I shook my head. "I don't know. Darren is going to freak." He already freaked, I thought, but didn't want to turn our mall trip into a bummer so I kept things light: "Guess where she was?" I paused for the full effect. "Partying with Corvette Kim."

He leaned his head back on the seat and laughed. "No shit?"

"Yeah."

"Well, that's Stacy. Darren knew she was kind of crazy when he first hooked up with her."

"Hopefully he'll remember that."

We walked into Serramonte through New York & Company. Serramonte is no Stonestown. No marble floors, no grand piano, no gleaming railings. Just a dirty, tiled fountain with a whole lot of loose change lying on the bottom, and enough Tagalog spoken by shoppers that the mall was sometimes called Little Manila.

We went straight to the ATM. "How much do you want?" I asked, punching in my PIN. "Sixty bucks? Eighty?"

"I didn't know I was hanging with Paris Hilton. Why not make it an even hundred?"

"Good idea," I said, but hesitated before selecting the amount of withdrawal. What if Darren changed his mind? Maybe he'd still need me. I hadn't even gotten my first paycheck yet. This was just old birthday money. I felt Jason watching over my shoulder and decided on eighty.

"I thought you were saving up to move out," Jason said, his eyes settling on me when I turned around. My face got hot.

"You know I made that crap up, right?" I stuffed the cash into my wallet. "I mean, obviously my parents would never let me go."

He shrugged. "I don't know. It could happen."

"Yeah, well. Not in my world." I started walking, my way of saying the subject was closed. "Where to?"

"Let's get some grub."

"I want to look at clothes first. It's always better to try on clothes before you eat."

"If you say so."

I dragged him into Express and pulled a bunch of clothes off the racks. When I got to the dressing room I looked at the clothes and I looked at me. Most of what I'd grabbed was pretty and trendy; clothes for the New Deanna. I stripped off my jeans and tank top and put on a pair of white capris and a fitted black T-shirt. I looked nice. Like a nice girl. Maybe if my dad saw me like that he'd change his mind about me. Maybe Jay would think differently, too. He'd see I could be a buddy and also girlfriend material. And when Lee got back and told him about what I'd said to her, he wouldn't take her side. He'd open his eyes and realize I had it all. He'd choose me.

I called through the dressing room door. "Are you out there?"

"Where else would I be?"

I straightened my hair, twisted it up into a bun, and stepped out of the dressing room with what I hoped was a sweet smile. "Hey, check me out."

Jason grinned. "That looks cute."

"Too bad I can't afford it, huh? Just the pants are, like, seventy."

He studied me and shrugged. "I don't know. It's not really you."

I forced myself to laugh. "Yeah." Back in the dressing room, I took my hair down, changed, and kicked the pants and shirt into a pile on the floor. I was still me, still stuck in my skin and the reality of my life. Pretty soon everything I had left would be gone: Darren and Stacy would either break up or move out without me, and Jason would pick Lee when he heard how shitty I'd been to her. I didn't even know if I'd be able to stay at

Picasso's after what had happened with Tommy. Even if I did stay, a crappy pizza place job being the best thing in my life was pretty sad.

I put on my game face and came out of the dressing room. "Let's go eat."

"I wish I had a food court in my house," Jason said, scanning our options.

"What do you want to eat?"

"Sbarro?"

"God no, please not pizza," I said. "Let's do Chinese."

We got in line at Panda Express and were checking out the menu when a voice behind us said, "Hey, Lambert, you want to go out with me? I've got two tickets to the parking lot behind Target."

It was Bruce Cowell, with Tucker Bradford tagging along like the second-string ass he was.

"I thought that was a special place just for you and your boyfriend," Jason said, pointing at Tucker.

Tucker stepped up. "I *know* I didn't hear that."

A couple of people in front of us turned around, pasty-looking office people whose lunch breaks we were about to ruin, or make exciting, depending how you looked at it.

I thought of a bunch of stuff I could say back to Bruce, but I was tired of it, tired of sticking up for myself and acting tough when all I wanted to do was disappear. I stared at the menu with my arms crossed and Jason turned his back on Tucker and Bruce. We got up to the counter. I ordered chow mein; Jason ordered a rice bowl. Suddenly Bruce's voice was right in my ear, whispering, "I guess this is a self-serve thing," and he put his hand between my legs from behind.

I spun around and pushed him as hard as I could, shouting, "Don't *ever* fucking touch me again!"

He ended up on the floor and just lay there, laughing. The office people looked away. Not one of them said *Hey, knock it off. What's your name? I'm going to call your parents.* They were afraid of us, scared we'd pull a gun on them and do some kind of mass murder in the mall.

Bruce kept laughing. Tucker danced around Jason, fists up like a boxer, going, "Right now, punk! Right now!"

A security guard came toward us fast. I grabbed Jason's shirt. "Let's *go*." We ran through the lunch crowd and into an elevator just before the doors closed. A mom with a stroller smiled at us, probably thinking we were just two crazy teenagers on a crazy teenage adventure. We all got out on the second floor; Jason and I went into Macy's, checking behind us for the rent-a-cop.

I kept it together, I did, until we got to the formal wear section, which was empty and quiet. Once I knew we were alone, I lost it. I sat on a pedestal at the feet of a mannequin in a tux, and cried.

Jason sat down next to me. "They're assholes," he said. "Forget them."

"He grabbed me," I said. "I'm not public property."

"Like I said. Assholes."

I couldn't believe I was crying *again,* more tears in two days than I'd cried in the last two years. I covered my face with one hand. "I was with Tommy last night."

"Tommy Webber?"

I nodded. "He works at Picasso's."

"Since when?"

"Since I started." I took my hand off my face and looked at Jason. I couldn't tell if he was disappointed or worried or jealous or what. "He gave me a ride home," I said, the tears slowing down to a trickle. "Nothing happened, really."

"Sorry, but I'm thinking *something* happened." Jason's voice was low. "Or else you wouldn't even be telling me this."

"Tommy was Tommy," I said. "I was me."

"That's not who you are, Deanna."

"We talked. Tommy and me, we talked about what happened . . . back then. I thought I felt better, but now . . ." Bruce's hand between my legs, right in front of a crowd of strangers, and worse, in front of Jason — it made a declaration about me: Deanna Lambert, you are just a skanky piece of ass. The tears started up again.

Jason stood. I thought he was going to walk away, which would pretty much seal it as my worst day ever. Instead, he did the most perfect thing, like we were in a movie: he took the handkerchief out of the mannequin's tux pocket and handed it to me. "You're not what Tommy says or what Bruce and Tucker say. Or what your dad says."

Him saying just the right thing like that, in a way it hurt

even more than if he'd walked away. I blew my nose and wiped my face. "Sometimes I think I am. But there's part of me that knows I'm not." A salesman came toward us and I crumpled the handkerchief into my fist.

"Can I help you?" he asked. "Are you all right?"

"Yeah, she's okay," Jason said.

"That's good, but this isn't a nightclub so find somewhere else to go, okay?"

We headed for the escalator and rode down, ending up in front of a giant wall of towels.

"How come . . ." I stopped myself.

"How come what?"

"Nothing."

"Dude. What?"

I put my hand between two pale blue towels. "How come you never asked me out?"

I think he shrugged. I don't know because I couldn't look at him.

"You're my friend. I never thought about you like that." He said it so easily and honestly that it shouldn't have made me feel bad, but it did.

"Never?"

"Nope."

"Not once," I said, playing with the terry-cloth loops of the towels, "in all this time you've known me, have you ever wondered what it would be like to kiss me?" I looked at him now, and watched his face turn a shade of red.

He half sat on a table of sale stuff. "Obviously I've wondered that. Guys wonder what it would be like to kiss *every* girl. Including their teachers."

"Eww."

"Okay, not *all* their teachers. I'm just saying there's curiosity and then there's what you would actually, seriously consider doing."

"And with me it's only . . . mild curiosity?"

"I didn't say 'mild.'"

"But you would never actually, seriously consider it?"

"Well, not *now*."

"Why not?" He gave me an embarrassed look, and I stumbled over my words. "I . . . well, obviously, there's *Lee*. I mean, I know that. I wasn't saying . . ."

"We're gonna miss the bus," he said. We walked out through Macy's and didn't talk while we waited. When the bus came, it was more crowded than it had been on the way over so we shared a double seat, me mortified at what I'd asked.

"We didn't even spend any money," I said, hoping I sounded more normal than I felt.

"Dang," Jason said. I could tell he was playing along, trying a little too hard to act like everything was okay.

I thought about how people probably thought we were boyfriend and girlfriend, and how if that were true maybe it would erase everything that happened with Tommy; I would just be a normal high school girl with a boyfriend.

"I don't want to go home," I said. I stared out at the stucco houses, the cars racing by us on the road. Fog rolled thick and white over the hills, tumbling into Pacifica right on schedule, like it just wouldn't be right for a whole eight hours of sun to shine on our stupid little town.

"You can come over if you want," Jason said. He might have sounded hesitant, or I might have been paranoid. "My mom could maybe give you a ride to work if she gets home in time."

We walked from the bus stop to his house, the fog feeling good at first, but by the time we got inside my arms were pink from the chill. Jason headed straight for the kitchen. "I'm starving." We never had eaten lunch. I watched my feet walk over the peach carpet, the path from the door to the kitchen worn thin.

He made a box of mac and cheese. We ate that and some brownies in front of the TV in his room. It felt normal again, already, like the conversation in Macy's had never happened.

His black sweatshirt, the one Lee always wore, hung on the back of a chair. I eyed it, imagining how it would be warm and soft with the smells of Jason and Lee mixed together: that citrusy smell of him and her bargain shampoo.

"Are you cold?" I asked. "I'm kind of cold."

"Oh." He dug around in his closet, barely taking his eyes off the TV, and handed me a clean flannel shirt that only smelled like laundry soap. I put it on over my tank top.

If I'd had a brain in my head I would have just relaxed, safe now in Jason's room, my favorite place to be. I should have been happy with what I had: a great friend, a place to be, a warm shirt. I could have wrapped myself in that feeling forever, or at least for another hour, maybe had a few more brownies to float away on a perfect cloud of sugar and TV and Jason. Instead, I asked: "If the stuff with Tommy had never happened, would you have asked me out?"

He half smiled, looking at me for a long time before saying, "There's no good answer to that question, right?"

I stared back, nervous and excited, like anything could happen. "Right."

We kept looking at each other until his phone rang. I jumped; he dove for it.

"Hello? Hey!" I watched his face change from whatever he'd been thinking the moment before to a sweet, happy grin. "How'd you find a phone?"

I knew it was Lee. My stomach clenched. I stood and went for the door.

"Where're you going?" Jason asked me. "Deanna's here," he said into the phone. "You want to talk to her?" He held the phone out to me, smiling. I pressed my back against the door and shook my head. He looked confused; I left the room, breathing hard and wondering what to do next, where to go. Work meant Tommy. Home meant maybe finding out Darren and Stacy were done. Just as my hand hit the front door, Jason came into the living room.

"What was that?" he asked. I didn't turn around. "She got all weird when I told her you were here."

"I gotta go."

"Nuh-uh." I felt his hand on my shoulder and turned around. He still had that confused expression, plus now he looked a little pissed. "So are you going to tell me, or what?"

We were close, there by the door, me in his shirt and his hand still warm on my shoulder. In my pocket was the handkerchief from the Macy's mannequin. I wished I could just hug him, the way Lee hugged me, easy and safe. But I didn't know how to do anything the easy and safe way.

"I could be your girlfriend," I said in a whisper. "I'd be a great girlfriend."

Jason looked at his shoes. "Yeah," he said. "I know."

And even though I knew that's not what he wanted, I kissed him. I put my arms around his neck and leaned into him with my whole body and kissed him. He hesitated, but only for a second, and kissed me back. It was just like I'd imagined, him pulling me closer and resting his hands on my hips, warmth spreading out from my belly.

Except there was Lee. Lee in my head, the way she looked at me the first time I'd told her about me and Tommy. The way her shrug was so sweet after everything I'd been hearing about myself for two years. *Hey, we all have stuff we want to change, right?*

I pulled myself away from Jason. He stared at the floor and shoved his hands into his pockets.

"How," I said, breaking down, *again*, "am I supposed to find my own way out?"

"What?"

"How am I supposed to find my own way out," I repeated, tears rolling down my face, "when every time I turn around . . . there's me?"

"You better go."

I opened the door and went out onto the front step. The fog was all the way in now, heavy and wet. I pulled Jason's shirt around me tighter.

9A.

If I ever met the girl on the waves, this is what I'd tell her:

Forgetting isn't enough.

You can paddle away from the memories and think they are gone.

But they will keep floating back, again and again and again.

They circle you, like sharks.

And you are bleeding your fear into the sea,

Until, unless

Something

Someone?

Can do more than just cover the wound.

10.

Tommy didn't show up to work. Brenda had stayed to cover for him, looking pissed as all hell to be there. Or maybe it was her really bad perm that made her so unhappy. I found Michael sitting in a booth, doing some paperwork in the dimness.

"Did he quit or what?" I asked.

Michael looked up and slid his glasses down to the tip of his nose. "Who, Tommy? I hope not. He said he was sick."

Brenda came over, tucking a towel into the side of her apron. "Did you tell her I can't close?"

"Not yet," Michael said, then turned to me. "Brenda can't close."

"My babysitter has to be home by ten," she explained. "Did

you tell her not to touch the register? Eight years and I've never been off by even one cent."

He smiled at her. "How 'bout you go and finish cleaning the slicer?" She walked off and Michael sighed. "Just stay off the cash register tonight. She has quite a little record going."

"She's worked here for eight years?"

"That's right."

"No offense," I said, "but if I'm still working here in eight years, just stab me."

He laughed. "Good plan. We should make a suicide pact."

Being around Michael relaxed me, so I stayed near his booth filling napkin holders and Parmesan shakers. At least work was something to do, somewhere to be, a place where I hadn't completely screwed anything up yet.

Jason said Lee got weird on the phone when she heard I was there; I wondered if it was because of our fight or because she worried that Jason and I might be messing around. Or both.

Had I really kissed him?

Or did he kiss me?

"Deanna?" Michael stood next to me lighting up a cigarette. "You've been standing there with that napkin holder for five minutes. It's starting to make me nervous."

"Sorry." I put the holder back and wiped down the table.

"You already wiped that table. Twice. Are you okay?"

I wanted to tell him to be careful being so nice to me or I might start crying yet again. "No."

Brenda called over to us from the register. "Hey, someone wants a pizza!"

"Imagine that," Michael said.

We got a little dinner rush, then it was dead again. My mom called at around eight, looking for me. "I didn't know where you were. It looks like you've been gone all day . . ." She actually sounded worried. "Stacy came back."

"I know." Brenda shot me a dirty look, as if I'd been talking on the phone for hours.

"You do? Oh. Well, it got a little loud with your father and your brother, then your brother and Stacy, then Stacy and your father . . . anyway, Stacy and Darren went for a drive and I've got April. Will you be able to get home all right?" Sure, Mom, I can just take care of myself. I've done such a good job of it so far. "Yeah."

"All right. Well, I'll see you later."

We were actually borderline busy the rest of the night; a softball team came in and stayed a couple of hours, drinking pitchers of beer and keeping the jukebox going. One gross guy with a hairy neck kept calling me "babe" and saying stuff like, "Hey, babe, if you work real hard maybe I'll give you a big tip." Brenda looked more and more pissed, like it was *my* fault some guy her age was hitting on me.

When the team got ready to leave, the guy gave me a napkin with his number on it and I made a big show of stuffing it into the bottom of a dirty beer glass. His friends laughed, but he got red and leaned close to me. "Bitch."

"You know what?" I said, ready to take him out with my tray. "I'm tired of people saying shit about me that isn't true. I've already knocked one guy on his ass today."

Michael came over and I figured he was going to drag me in the back and fire me. Instead, he told the guy to get out. "And don't come back," he said. "I don't need your business." Which was bull. The guy flipped Michael off and walked out with the team. My hands shook. I knew I should thank Michael, but I finished clearing tables and did the dishes without a word.

When Brenda left at nine thirty, Michael put out the "closed" sign even though it said right on the door that we were open until eleven. We worked fast, putting food away in the walk-in and scrubbing the counters down. I mopped the floors and he cleaned the bathrooms and then we did some prep for the next day. When everything was done, Michael said, "So. What was all that about?"

"The guy was a jerk."

"Uh-huh," he said, nodding. "Just a run-of-the-mill jerk. Not worth your time or energy, really."

I leaned against the sink. "I should get home."

"Yeah, looks like you can hardly wait."

I stared at the floor for a while, not wanting to talk, not wanting to leave. "Am I in trouble?"

"With me? No." He tucked his glasses into his shirt pocket. "I'm not in any hurry, you know."

The way he said that, I knew I could talk to him. He wasn't

all wannabe guidance counselor, going *sometimes it helps to talk* and *how does that make you feel?*

"Last night," I said, taking a deep breath. "I did something really stupid. Or at least half stupid."

"Okay."

"Today . . ." I didn't want to cry anymore. Michael waited. "Today I screwed up again."

"Mm."

"Like I do all the time."

"All the time?"

"Yeah."

"Well," he said. "I kind of doubt you screw up *all* the time."

"Okay," I said. "A lot. There has to be a limit, right? How many screw-ups do you get before you're out?"

He stroked his mustache. The walk-in hummed behind us. "Good question. I'm . . . let's see . . . forty-six. I guarantee you that I've screwed up more than you have, and I'm still in the game."

I studied him: just a nice middle-aged guy with his own business. He got along all right. "Have you ever done something shitty to a friend?" I asked.

"Yes," he said.

"I mean, *really* shitty?"

"You doubt me? Let's examine the evidence: I dropped out of Stanford my sophomore year. For no good reason, mind you. I was just tired of homework. You can imagine how my parents felt about that. Then I got married and divorced —

twice — before figuring out that I like men." His voice got quiet. "I loved my wives. Dearly. Talk about doing something shitty to a friend."

"Yeah," I said. "That's pretty bad."

"Thanks. But enough about me."

"I just need to get out of Pacifica."

Michael nodded. "And you will, eventually. Only, don't mistake a new place for a new you. I've done that more than once. You asked me before why I stay here. Maybe that's why," he said, "now that I think about it. Might as well deal with myself right here. It's as good a place as any." He took out a cigarette and put it between his lips. "And as for that friend. It's worth it to say sorry. Even if he doesn't want to hear it."

"She."

He reached into his pocket for a lighter. "So do you want a ride home?"

"Yeah." I put Jason's shirt on over my Picasso's tee. "Thanks."

Darren's car sat parked in front of the house, the light from the living room spilling out into the driveway, a few of the Christmas bulbs flickering on and off. I stood in front of the door wondering what I'd find when I got inside. My dad walked by the window and I stepped into the shadow of the house so he wouldn't see me. I couldn't bear to go in and hear his version of what had happened with Stacy.

I walked around to the side of the house. My feet got tangled in an old garden hose but otherwise I didn't make a sound. I always kept my bedroom window open a little so that I could smell the salty fog at night. I worked it up slowly and climbed in, landing on my bed. For a long time, I lay there with the light off, Jason's shirt wrapped around me.

It's times like this a person wants a friend, I thought, someone you can call no matter what time it is and tell the whole story, your own version, and know that you've got someone on your side. Who, I wondered, would be on my side now?

It had always been Darren, and I knew that in the end he was the only other person in the world who knew what it was like to be a Lambert. I couldn't stay mad at him. He was only trying to do what was right for him and Stacy and April. After everything that had happened I at least needed to see Darren's face before I went to sleep.

I pushed open my bedroom door a little and listened. The TV in Mom and Dad's room was on, the rest of the house now dark. I crept through the hall and put my ear to the basement door before going down the stairs as quietly as I could, circling the room by the light that came in through the ground-level window.

Darren was there in the bed, lying on his stomach and snoring softly.

No Stacy, no April.

I touched April's little Minnie Mouse crib sheet, then went over to sit on the edge of Darren's bed. He turned over, opened his eyes, and sat up quick.

"God," he said, flopping back down after seeing it was just me. "You scared the hell out of me."

"Where are they?"

"I'll tell you tomorrow. I gotta sleep."

"Are they coming back?"

"Deanna . . ."

"Just tell me."

"Let me sleep, okay? I'll talk to you tomorrow." He rolled over and pulled the covers up to his chin, the same way he used to sleep when we were kids, camping out in the living room or backyard.

There were things I thought in my head while I looked at him but couldn't say — things like:

I'm glad you're back, Darren.

Sorry about yesterday.

Darren, I understand what you have to do.

I tucked the corner of the blanket under the mattress, careful not to touch him, and then went up to bed.

I woke up early after a bad night's sleep. Mom was in the pink kitchen in her fuzzy pink robe, making coffee the way she always had: scooping coffee grounds, pouring water, and flicking on the switch in a few quick movements.

"You're up," she said. "We didn't hear you get in last night."

"You must have been asleep already."

"It's possible. Yesterday just went on forever."

Slight understatement. "Where are Stacy and April?"

"Oh honey, it's a long story. Why don't you have some breakfast first? How about oatmeal? It's a good morning for oatmeal . . ." She was already getting out an envelope of instant oatmeal and a bowl.

"I'm not hungry yet. I just want to know where they are."

She opened the envelope anyway, and emptied it into the bowl. "You should really ask your brother for the details. It's hard for young parents, you know. They'll work it out. Is cinnamon-raisin okay?"

"God, Mom. I don't want any oatmeal."

"Well, all right, you don't have to snap at me."

I went to the fridge for a can of root beer and Dad walked in, took his National Paper Company mug off the hook on the wall, and poured his coffee.

"Where were you last night?" he asked.

"Work."

"I didn't hear you come in."

Mom piped up: "We must have been asleep, honey."

"How did you get home?"

I cracked open my root beer and sipped it. I knew the conversation wasn't going to go anywhere good but I went along with it anyway. "My boss gave me a ride."

Mom looked at me like I should have known better, like I should have lied, then she hovered around Dad. "I was just telling Deanna it's a good morning for oatmeal. Do you want some? It'll just take me five minutes."

· 156 ·

He ignored her. "And your boss's name is . . . ?"

"Michael."

"We have cinnamon-raisin, and apple-cinnamon . . . hmm, they all seem to have cinnamon . . ." She held the box in her hands, looking back and forth between Dad and me like she would have started tap dancing and juggling the oatmeal packets if she thought it would help.

"And how old is this Michael?"

"Old," I said. "Forty-six."

Dad's jaw started working and he put down his mug. "And why is he giving you rides?"

"Because he's nice," I said. I sipped my root beer and stared Dad down. "Plus I fucked him."

Mom gasped. "Deanna!"

Dad turned red and pointed his finger at me. "If you think that's funny . . ."

Darren walked in right then and went straight for the coffeepot. He filled a cup and saw Mom, still holding the box of oatmeal. "I'll have some oatmeal."

"Not now, Darren," she said.

"I don't think it's funny," I said. "I think it sucks. I think it sucks that you think I would actually sleep with my forty-six-year-old boss. It sucks that's what you think!" I'd started crying, of course.

Darren looked confused. "Isn't your boss gay?"

Dad turned to Darren, then back to me. "Is he?"

"I guess," I said.

Mom gave a nervous laugh. "Why didn't you *say* so?"

"What if he wasn't?" I said. "If he wasn't, what would you think? That I let him feel me up for a free pizza?"

Dad lowered his voice, eyes locked on mine, like we were the only ones in the room. "It's not as if I don't have reason to wonder."

And this was it. I could almost feel it, like an audible click, the house and us in it finally latching onto the tracks, taking us wherever it was we'd been needing to go. This was the thing we had all known was going to happen sooner or later, the thing we'd spent three years trying to avoid.

"You're always going to hate me," I said, really sobbing now, "for something I did when I was thirteen?"

"Your father does not *hate* you!" Mom said, slamming the box of oatmeal down on the counter, showing more feeling of any kind than I'd seen from her in a long time.

"That's what you think?" Dad asked, looking like he could cry, too. "You think I hate you?"

"What's she supposed to think, Dad?" Darren said.

We all looked at him and I flashed on something, I understood that this wasn't only about me and Dad, or me and Tommy. Mom and Darren, even Stacy, even April, Lee, Jason, and now Michael . . . we were all part of this thing that had happened, two people in the back seat of a classic Buick, doing something private, only not private, because there was a crowd on this train that had in fact been in motion for a long time now.

"Ray," Mom said, turning to Dad, "say something."

"What? What am I supposed to say?"

Darren and I watched Mom, me trying to stifle my sobs to something less animal-like.

"Tell her you love her," Mom whispered. "Tell her."

"I . . . of course." Dad looked at me. My dad, my father. He wanted to say it, I knew. "It's . . ." His hands dropped to his sides, and he walked out of the kitchen. A few seconds later we heard the front door open and close, then the sound of the car starting and pulling away.

I went to the sink and took a couple of paper towels off the roll to blow my nose and wipe my eyes. Mom sank into a kitchen chair and sighed. "Well. You shouldn't have talked to your father like that, Deanna. I don't know why you had to use that language." She lifted a hand and ran it over the Formica surface of the table. "It's hard for him, honey. It always has been."

I held my root beer to my throbbing temple. "I know."

She got up and came toward me like she might hug me or at least put her arm around my shoulders. Instead she stopped in front of me and shook her head, speaking quietly: "But it's no excuse, is it," she said, shaking her head. "It's no excuse." She poured herself another cup of coffee and stared out the window.

"Come on," Darren said to me, pulling my arm.

I followed him downstairs. My head felt full and huge from crying so hard; my throat ached and I could only breathe through my mouth. I sat on Darren's bed with a box of tissues.

"Are you okay?" he asked.

"Did that actually happen?" I was disoriented, still thinking about the shock on Dad's face when I'd said what I did, and that denying he hated me might be the best he could do, might be as close to a declaration for me that he was able to give.

"I think so." He sat next to me. "I mean, holy shit, I think it really did."

I blew my nose a few more times. "So," I said, ready to think about something else for a minute. "Where are they?"

"At Stacy's mom's."

"I thought they hated each other."

"They do."

"When are they coming back?"

"I don't know. April will be back tomorrow for a couple of days. Stacy wants to come back, too." He ran his hand over his hair. "I told her I'd think about it."

"What do you mean, you'll *think* about it?" I couldn't believe he didn't feel the shift in our little universe the way I did, the way everything was connected, the way we all had to be if there was any chance for us.

"She left me!" he said. "She *left* me and April."

"She came back."

Darren shook his head. "I just don't know if that's who I want for the mother of my baby."

I laughed, even though it made my head throb. "Too late, dumbass, she *is* the mother of your baby. You think you're going to go out and just round up some other chick to be April's mom?"

"Maybe. I don't know." He stood up and stripped his T-shirt off. "I gotta get in the shower."

I stayed in his room and crawled into the bed. It was still warm where he'd slept. My head hurt so bad from crying and when I thought about Jason and Lee and what Darren had just said, it hurt even more, but I knew, I *knew*, that even if Darren hadn't felt it, the shift of things, that I had. That something had happened.

After he showered, he came out of the bathroom with a towel wrapped around his waist. "Um, a little privacy?"

"I'm not going to watch. God." I turned over so my back was to him and stared at the wall. "You have to call her," I said. "And tell her to come back."

"Well I don't know if I'm ready to do that."

"So?" I could see it all so clearly, the way it had to be.

"I can't just let her get away with it, Deanna."

"Why not?" I said. "Just call her and say you're sorry and you want her to come home."

"*I'm* sorry?"

"Yeah." I traced my finger along a crack in the basement wall. "For not trying to understand why she left and for kicking her out and everything."

"What about her? She's the one who left!"

I turned back over and looked at Darren. He had on his pants and shirt. "Did she say sorry?"

He looked down, picked his Safeway jacket up off the floor. "Yeah. But I don't know if that's enough."

"What else is there?" I was going to have to tell Lee what I'd done. I would have to face her, and confess.

"Well, you know, she has to, like, prove that she's going to be a good mother and not do that again."

I handed him a pair of socks out of the pile on the bed. "Like Dad wants me to prove I'm not who he thinks I am?"

He took the socks from me and held them in his hands. "I'm not like Dad."

"If you say so."

11.

I took a shower and some aspirin, ate a grilled cheese sandwich. I was exhausted and alone. I called Jason's cell and got his voice mail. "Call me," I said.

The phone rang about twenty minutes later and I grabbed it, hoping for Jason but getting Michael. He asked if I could come in early because Brenda's babysitter was sick. I waited around a while in case Jason called, then got a bus down to Picasso's.

Michael and I spent most of the afternoon cleaning the pizza oven and the walk-in. "One more citation from the board of health," he said, "and I'm out of business. Which wouldn't be the worst thing in the world." He handed me a crock of sliced tomatoes that had practically turned to mush. "Here, throw this in the minestrone pot."

What Michael called "minestrone" was really a slimy mixture of leftover pizza sauce and water and vegetables from the salad bar that were about to go bad, with some macaroni thrown in. I added the tomatoes.

"I'm off for a smoke break," he said. "Back in five."

"What happened to just smoking in here?"

"I'm turning over a new leaf."

While Michael was out, Tommy showed up. He went straight into the back for his apron and started rolling out pizza crusts. I remembered his face looking out across the top of his car in the old Chart House parking lot, confused, even innocent, in a way.

"Aren't you going to say hi to me," I said, imitating him.

"Hi." He looked up and smiled a little, then went back to rolling his crusts. I watched him, trying to find that place in myself I always went to when faced with Tommy Webber. It wasn't there; something was missing. "Take a picture," he said, "it'll last longer."

"I think that's enough crusts," I said.

He flipped his hair out of his eyes and kept rolling. "I don't remember Michael making you the boss."

"Oh, *you're* going to be mad at *me* now? Whatever."

A few people phoned in orders for pickup and an older couple came in, so we kept busy for a little while. I was in the back running some dishes through the washer when Michael came to tell me I had visitors.

Darren and Stacy and April were there, standing at the front counter.

Honestly? I'd been expecting them. It was inevitable, almost, after what had gone on in the Lambert kitchen that morning. Still, the sight of Stacy smiling and holding onto April was a major Hallmark moment and almost made me miss the fact that Darren's eyes were fixed on Tommy, who stood there looking like he wasn't sure if he should grin or run.

I came around the counter and pulled Darren's arm. "Yeah, he works here, okay? Let's go sit down."

"What the hell, Deanna?" Darren muttered as we took a booth.

"It's cool," I said. "Trust me."

I took April from Stacy and blew a raspberry into her neck. "You guys want pizza?" I asked.

"No, thanks," said Stacy.

She leaned against Darren and watched April in my arms and I felt happy, really and truly happy, like I'd done something good talking to Darren that morning the way I did. It felt like the best thing I'd done in my life, maybe.

Darren stared at me. "Why didn't you tell me he worked here?"

"Because she knew you'd freak out, I'm guessing," Stacy said.

"You'd be right," Darren said. "If he touches you, Deanna, his ass is grass."

"I'll make a note of that." Darren would never know how I'd gone off with Tommy one more time. Somehow I was sure it wasn't something Tommy would spread around, not this time.

It got quiet for a minute, and awkward, then April made this growling sound and we all cracked up. "She just started doing that yesterday," Stacy said.

Everything with babies happened so fast. I tried not to think about all the stuff I'd miss when Darren and Stacy left.

"We better go," Darren said.

"Already?"

"Stacy has to work. We just thought we should come by, you know, so you could see."

Stacy took April from me and smiled. "I'll pick you up after work, okay?"

"Yeah," I said.

I watched them leave and everything felt possible. If I could have called Lee that second and told her everything, I would have.

Tommy came up to me. "So is Darren going to beat my head in?"

"Not unless I want him to," I said. I looked at Tommy's little grin and his scar and I knew what was different.

"What?" he asked. "Why are you looking at me like that?"

"I just figured something out."

"What?"

"I don't hate you anymore," I said. "Something about you still pisses me off, but I don't hate you." It was weird, almost sad, like a part of me was gone.

"Wow. I feel so special."

"Break it up, kids," Michael was saying. "We have customers."

Stacy picked me up right on time, looking the same as ever behind the wheel of the Nova, except for her red hair. We rolled out of the lot and through the dark streets. I leaned my head against the cool window and closed my eyes, exhaustion hitting me all at once.

"You okay?" Stacy asked.

"Yeah. Long day."

"I heard what happened with your dad this morning."

"It was crazy."

"Wish I'd been there."

I think I dozed off, for a minute or two at least, because before I knew it the car had stopped and there we were at the house. Stacy turned off the engine but didn't move to get out. "Deanna," she said, "Darren told me what you said. About . . . me. Us. He listens to you, you know. He respects you."

"Darren? Respects *me*?"

"He doesn't say it like that. But I can tell." She checked herself in the rearview mirror, tucking a piece of hair behind her ear. "That's why he gets on you about stuff like college. He knows you could really do it."

I thought about that: me, in college, sitting there taking notes and buying take-out coffee in between classes.

"Anyway," Stacy said, "thanks. What I did was dumb. I know that."

"Well," I said, trying to remember the exact words Lee had said to me when we first met, "we all have stuff we wish we could change. Right?"

She laughed. "Damn straight."

We sat in the car a few minutes more and I let myself imagine, one last time, what it would have been like for me and Stacy and Darren to have a new life, together: me waking up some Saturday morning and walking into a sunny kitchen, where Stacy would be feeding April in a high chair. Darren would be by the coffeepot, and would turn to me when I came in, *Hey, Deanna, what's on for today?* I'd pour my own cup of coffee and lean against the counter. *A little homework,* I'd say, *then I'm free until work tonight.* We'd make a plan, maybe, to divide up the weekend chores, then do some errands together and grab a burrito in the city before going our separate ways.

I let myself picture it all.

Then I let it go.

And I opened the car door, and Stacy and I went inside the house, the actual house, where in a way we *did* have our own little family, not a made-up one that only existed in my head, but a real one where at least Darren and Stacy and me had figured something out. Somehow we had found our own small island of declaration for each other.

12.

I slept until eleven-thirty the next morning, and woke up feeling like I could sleep even more. But I had things to do.

First: I called Jason.

"I think I'm going to tell her," I said.

There was a long pause before he answered, "*Why?*"

"Because. I just have to."

"Dude. Do you mean, like, tell her *everything?*"

"Yes." I'd thought it all out. Getting the truth into the wide open was the only thing that worked with Tommy, the thing that got my dad to finally *look* at the way it was, the thing that had brought Stacy and Darren back together. It had to work with Lee, too.

"Please," Jason said, "I beg you, just leave that one little part out."

"Trust me. Lee's into honesty. That kind of stuff matters a lot to her."

"And I'm into keeping my girlfriend."

"You didn't do anything wrong."

Jason was quiet for a second. "Yeah I did."

I thought about the way he'd held me when I kissed him, how he'd pulled me closer, kissed back. Picturing us together like that made me teeter, just a little, before I refocused. "Well, I'll just tell her my part."

"Holy crap, you're serious."

"Don't worry, okay?"

He sighed and I thought I could hear him open a door, like he was standing in the kitchen, maybe, staring into the cupboard looking for a snack. "The whole thing was weird," he said. "It's like it never happened."

"It did, though."

"But why do you have to tell her?"

I sighed. "I know it sounds like a bad idea." I didn't know how to explain that, for me, it was the only option.

"Good luck."

Second: I cleaned my room. I took down my macaroni-art turkey. I picked up my clothes. I organized my CDs. I cleaned off my desk, then I pulled the comp book out from behind my bed and set it by the desk lamp, where it would be waiting for me when I needed it.

Third: I found Stacy in the kitchen, trying to fix herself a bowl of cereal while balancing April on her hip.

"Need help?"

She handed April over. "Thanks. Just trying to eat before *she* wants to eat again. I think she's having a growth spurt or something."

I sat down with April and turned her to face me. She smiled her gummy smile and I squeezed her chubby legs. I took a deep breath. "I decided . . . that I want to give you guys everything I make this summer. So that you can move out."

Stacy put down her spoon. "No way, Deanna. That's your money."

I held April to me and smelled her hair, fruity and milky and dusty all at once. "If you guys move out, that means I'll have a place to go, too. Once in a while, I mean. To visit. So in a way I'd be using the money on something for me."

"Deanna, we couldn't. Anyway, Darren would never let you."

"It's my money, not Darren's." April looked up at me and flapped her arms.

Stacy shoveled a spoonful of cereal into her mouth, shaking her head. "You better just leave me out of it, because I'd probably say yes."

I was off work that night and didn't know what to expect with Dad and me both home. Mom had left a note for me to put a casserole in the oven, so I did, and set the table for four. Stacy left for her shift, and Darren came home from his.

"What are you doing?" he asked, appearing in the kitchen, carrying April in her car seat. He took in the set table, complete with water glasses and cloth napkins.

"Um, making dinner?"

We looked at each other and both came out with the same nervous laughter. Darren ran his hand through his hair. "Why the hell not, huh? This family has done crazier things than eat dinner together. I'm in."

When Mom got home from work and found us there, her tired face lifted. "You kids are both in tonight? That smells wonderful, Deanna."

"You made it, Mom. I just put it in the oven."

"I can take over from here," she said, setting her purse down and rolling up her sleeves.

"It's okay," Darren said. "We got it covered."

She smiled. "All right. Maybe I'll go put my feet up for a bit."

The casserole finished, Darren threw some frozen rolls into the toaster oven, and we waited fifteen minutes past the time Dad usually got home from work. "Maybe he's working over-time," Darren said.

"They never give him overtime," I said, unwrapping a stick of butter and putting it in the butter dish we hadn't used since Thanksgiving.

"Well, I'm starving, so let's get the show on the road." He

put April's car seat on a chair so she could watch us eat. I brought everything to the table. Mom came in and sat down, checking her watch.

Then we all heard the front door open and close, and he walked in.

April flapped her arms.

Dad stopped, and I imagined us through his eyes — his family, sitting in a pink kitchen: his tired wife, who never complained; his son who looked exactly like him; his daughter, who used to be the baby, his baby girl; and now April, his granddaughter, who had a whole life in front of her, with no real mistakes in it yet. Could he look at us someday, I wondered, maybe today, and not be disappointed? Could he see us, and himself, for who we really were?

He sat down.

Mom dished up the casserole.

I passed the butter.

April watched us with her big eyes.

The Lamberts, eating dinner.

Before bed, I wandered into the living room to find Mom still up and watching *Letterman.* She smiled at me and held out a bag of microwave popcorn. I sat next to her, taking a big handful.

Her legs were stretched out onto the coffee table, stubbly

hair all over, like she hadn't had time to shave for maybe a week. "I'm going to stay up all night watching TV and then call in sick tomorrow," she said.

"Sounds like a plan."

A commercial came on and I felt Mom's eyes on me. "Come here, sweetheart. Snuggle up." She held her arm out, smiling. I was embarrassed; I hadn't cuddled with Mom since I was a kid, way before Tommy. But the living room was dark except for the TV and it was just the two of us, so I leaned toward her and she pulled me in. She smelled like popcorn and the flowery lotion she always used. I curled my legs underneath me, putting my head in her lap.

She stroked my hair while we finished up *Letterman* and the popcorn. Then I closed my eyes, concentrating on the warmth of her fingers on my scalp, the worn chenille of her old robe under my cheek. Tears gathered behind my eyes; I sniffled, hoping Mom wouldn't say anything or ask anything or stop touching my hair. She didn't.

I lay there in my mom's lap for I don't know how long, and before I drifted to sleep I thought of something Lee said once when she was talking about church, that sometimes there was no reason to believe in God and you'd look at your life and know it was crazy to feel peaceful but you did anyway, and that was faith. I know that having faith in your family isn't the same as God or religion or whatever, but I could kind of get what Lee meant about believing in something when it made more sense not to.

13.

For the rest of the week, we were pretty much back to our routine: Darren would get home from work, do a couple of errands with Stacy. Mom would come home and start dinner, then Stacy and I left for work, us pulling out as Dad pulled in.

I spent a lot of my time working out what I'd say to Lee. It felt exciting and nerve-wracking all at once, this big important thing that I wanted to do right. I played it all out in my head, the words I'd use and the different things she might say back . . . what I would do if she refused to listen.

I had it all under control, I thought.

What actually happened was this:

Lee called me the day after she got back from camping.

"Hey," she said, sounding not exactly like herself. Which wasn't surprising, considering our last conversation.

I'd assumed I'd be the one calling her when I was ready; I didn't think she'd call me. "Hi."

"So, I'm back," she said. "Obviously."

Awkward pause.

"How was it?"

"Okay. If you don't mind giant mosquitoes and spiders and digging holes whenever you have to go to the bathroom."

Now, Deanna, I told myself. Jump in anytime.

But Lee kept talking. "Me and Jay are going to Taco Bell. In, like, twenty minutes. Can you meet us?"

I hesitated. Maybe my memory of our fight was different than hers. Maybe I hadn't been as much of a bitch as I thought. "Um, yeah. I'll be there."

My heart pounded as I got ready. On the bus down to the beach, I ran through the script in my mind, remembering all my main points, like:

1. *I was sorry about what I said at the pizza place, that I wasn't a friend when she needed me to be*
2. *It was just both our bad luck that I was having the worst week of my life when everything happened*
3. *Kissing Jason was stupid, stupid, stupid and I didn't mean anything by it and I'd never do it again, and I knew honesty was important to her and I just wanted everything out in the open*

The thing was, it all sounded like bullshit.

I got off the bus and crossed the highway to the Taco Bell on the beach, the nicest Taco Bell in the history of Taco Bells, with a fireplace and a deck overlooking the Pacific, and a window where surfers could walk up and order without having to change out of their dripping wet suits.

I could see them inside, Lee and Jason, standing around looking up at the menu board. I opened the door. Lee walked over to me, but stopped short of hugging. She looked different: she had a little tan and her hair had grown some.

"Hi," she said.

"Hi."

Jason nodded his head. "Hey."

It was the first time I'd seen him since that day at his house. I still had his shirt. "Hi."

"Let's get, like, a *lot* of food," Lee said, turning back to the menu. Abruptly, maybe, or maybe I imagined it. "Half our food went bad on the camping trip and my stepdad kept using the phrase 'meal rations.' It got a little desperate."

We ordered and sat out on the deck. I kept thinking about what to say and when to say it, but Lee talked almost nonstop about her trip: swimming in the Russian River, the sheep that showed up at their campsite every morning, her leaky air mattress. "I already suggested a new family tradition that involves staying home and watching TV . . ." She pushed her quesadilla toward me. "Have some. It's yummy."

"Thanks."

Jason kept his eyes on his food, mostly. Either that or watching the surfers, not looking at Lee, not leaning into her, not reaching over for her food the way he usually did.

"How's work?" Lee asked. "You know, the Tommy situation and everything."

"It's . . . it's fine. We worked it out."

"Really? That's cool." She shoveled more food in, still talking fast. "How much have you saved up? When are you moving out?"

"Oh. I'm not. Not this year."

She didn't seem surprised. "Drag. Maybe next summer?"

"Maybe."

The wind kicked up and blew our chips off the table and onto the deck. Seagulls swooped down and fought each other for the food. "Shit!" Lee said, jumping up and kicking in the direction of the gulls. "Get away, you piece of shit shit-ass birds! God, I *hate* you!"

My eyes met Jason's. Something had happened. I didn't know what, but something, because Lee a) rarely swore, and b) didn't get upset over little stuff, ever. Jason looked away, and got up to dump his trash.

Lee came back and sat at the table. Her eyes welled up.

"Lee . . . ," I started, helpless.

"Don't," she whispered. "Just don't say anything." She lifted her head, looked right at me. "It's okay," she said, quietly. "It's okay." She wiped her sleeve across her face. "Let's get some of those cinnamon thingies. I'm still hungry."

. . .

Jason called about an hour after I got home.

"Hey," he said. I pictured him in his room, stretched out on the bed with clothes piled all over and old bowls covered with food crust on the floor next to him. "Don't be mad at me," he said.

"Why would I be?"

"I know you wanted to tell her yourself so I'm sorry, but I had to. I felt like I was about to puke all the time until I told her."

My stomach dropped and my heart sped up. "Wait. What?"

"I know I was the one who didn't want to tell her in the first place, but I had to."

I closed my eyes and pressed the phone to my ear until it hurt. "When?" I asked. "When did you tell her?"

"Yesterday. She called me when she got back and I kind of let it all out." He sighed. "I know. I'm an idiot."

She knew. She'd known when she called me, she'd known at Taco Bell, she'd known when she looked at me and said, *It's okay*.

"I . . . I don't get it."

"Yeah. Well. Me neither. That's just Lee."

"I gotta go." I hung up on Jason and sat on my bed. How could she do that? What kind of a person just said, *Yeah, okay, you kissed my boyfriend. It's cool.* What did it mean? Were we still friends? We couldn't be, I thought, there was no way. Not now that she knew the truth.

I got under the covers on my bed, pulled them all the way up over my head, and cried.

14.

After work that night while closing up with Michael, I found Tommy mopping the men's room.

"Hey," I said. "Can I talk to you?"

"Go ahead."

"Okay. Look at me."

He looked at me and leaned on the mop. "Yes?"

"It's *okay*," I said. "I mean, as in, I forgive you, or whatever."

He laughed. "What? What'd I do now?"

"I *forgive* you," I repeated. "It's okay. For everything before. You said you're sorry, and now I'm saying . . . it's okay."

"Okaaay." He went back to mopping.

"Do you feel any different?"

"Yeah. I feel horny."

"Be serious for one second. Do you feel different?"

"I guess," he said, wringing the mop. "Yeah. I kinda do."

"You do?" He looked serious, but I just never knew with Tommy.

"Well, you mean it, right? You're not just yanking my chain?"

I thought about it. He'd apologized, and I believed he meant it. I could look at him and not hate him. What else was there to consider? "I mean it."

"Okay, then, yeah. I feel different."

"Different how?"

He slapped the mop back onto the floor and swished it around. "Different like I don't have to feel like a piece of shit every time you look at me."

"Well, that's something."

Maybe that's all there was to it. Except Tommy had said he was sorry to me, and I'd never had the chance to say that to Lee. Not yet.

Every day, I woke up thinking it would be the day I would call Lee. I'd call her and say what I needed to say, and then things could get back to normal. But every day, I didn't call her. And I didn't call Jason, even when his messages piled up. And then July turned into August, and every day the feeling that it was too late grew and grew.

One night Darren picked me up from work when I was expecting Stacy. "We need to talk," he said.

I prepared myself for the Big Talk, the one about how he and Stacy were ready to move out and they loved me and everything but of course we all understood I had to keep living with Mom and Dad. It was okay, I was ready for it.

"How come you don't talk to Lee anymore?" Darren asked, surprising me.

I could have given him some crap-ass excuse about being busy but he'd see through it. "I kissed Jason while she was camping."

"You *kissed* Jason?" Darren sounded shocked, which made me feel sort of good, like he knew that wasn't who I was, not who I really am.

"And Lee found out."

"How?"

"Jason told her."

"Brilliant." Darren sighed and we drove up into the hills, away from our house. "So you'll make up."

I looked at him. "What would *you* do if your best friend kissed Stacy?"

"Okay, *my* best friend kissed my little sister," he said. "But it's different. Me and Tommy were drug buddies. You and Lee and Jason, you're for real."

"Well, Lee actually, like, *forgave* me or whatever." I hated to even say the word. "But she has to. I don't think she's allowed to stay mad at me. It's against her religion or something."

"And you're going to turn that down?" He laughed, shaking his head. "God, do you even *remember* what you said to me that morning? When I was going to string Stacy along a few weeks on account of her leaving?" He glanced at me. "I thought you had it all together with that stuff, Deanna. You actually sounded like you knew what the hell you were talking about."

"Well I guess I didn't," I said. "Anyway, that's different. You guys have April."

"Oh, so it's okay for *you* to turn out like Dad?"

We cruised over the top of Crespi Drive. The night was clear and you could see the blue-black of the ocean under the moon.

"All I'm saying is look at him, right?" Darren continued. "He can't forgive you, or me, or Stacy, or the paper company, not really. Or himself, you know? He can't get past any of it and actually live a life. He can barely sit at the dinner table with all of us without looking like he's gonna have a stroke."

I laughed. "Yeah."

"So don't go thinking you're special or different, that if you let this thing with Lee just stay like it is that it won't hurt you."

"*Okay,* Dr. Phil. I get it." We circled around and headed back down into the valley. I knew Darren was right, but it was harder than he made it sound. I could even understand, just a little, how it was easier for my dad to cut people off and shut himself down than to do what it took to make things right.

Still, every day turned into the next without me making a single step.

. . .

Darren did eventually get around to the Big Talk. He called me down to the basement when he and Stacy were both there and told me they were getting ready to move out. They already had some empty cardboard boxes from Safeway sitting around the room. Even though I saw it coming and thought I was ready, it still made me feel like I'd slipped from a high cliff, not sure where I'd land.

"It's kind of a dump," he was saying, "but we're taking it."

"I have almost five hundred dollars saved," I said. "Like I said before, I want to give it to you."

Darren shook his head. "And like *I* said, no."

"It's my money."

"Yeah," Stacy said, "it's her money." April sat in her lap, sucking on her little fist and watching us.

"Yeah, and it's going to stay your money," Darren said. "Use it for college, okay? Or something. Hell, maybe you want to take a road trip after you graduate or move to New York or something, I don't know, but don't give it to us."

"You can't afford to move without it," I said, seeing the last shred of my fantasy blowing away. I knew I had to let it.

"Yeah, we can. It's called a cash advance and there are five credit card companies dying to give me one."

Stacy sighed. She'd bleached her hair again, but there was still an orange-gold tint left over from the Copper Sunset. "Darren, we talked about that."

He waved his hand at her. "Yeah, yeah. I know. But we'll pay it off fast. I'll work overtime." Darren put his hand on my shoulder, the closest he'd ever come to hugging me. "Look, you don't have to pay us to not forget about you."

Stacy eyed me and said, "Come here."

I got off the floor and sat on the edge of the bed next to her. She put her arm around me, tough Stacy, who used to scare the hell out of me in the halls of Terra Nova. "You can keep a toothbrush at our place, okay?"

It was really going to happen. I nodded and tried not to cry.

"Yeah," Darren said. "Think of all the free babysitting you'll do."

I forced a smile. "We'll see."

15.

One morning in August, I walked in on my dad in the kitchen. He looked up and then back at the coffeepot. This is how it had been for weeks: us avoiding each other, tiptoeing around the house, peeking around corners to make sure the other wasn't there. I went past him and got down a box of cereal and a bowl. I poured the milk and turned around. Dad was standing there holding a spoon, which he held out to me. "Here."

I took it and sat down. He stayed standing with his National Paper mug, eyes on the floor. "So school starts soon I guess," he said.

"Yeah. Two more weeks." I watched him, in his striped auto parts shirt and fresh crew cut, looking like Darren.

"Well. You get some tough classes junior year, right? Might be hard to keep your grades where you had them."

"Maybe."

He dumped out his coffee and rinsed the mug, placing it carefully on the hook near the sink. "Your mom said you've been saving your paychecks. Maybe we can find you an old car."

He walked out of the kitchen without waiting for my reply, back straight.

I smiled.

A spoon held out. A question about school. The possibility of an old car.

It came down to the smallest things, really, that a person could do to say I'm sorry, to say it's okay, to say I forgive you. The tiniest of declarations that built, one on top of the other, until there was something solid beneath your feet. And then . . . and then. Who knew?

When I finished my cereal, I took a piece of the scratch paper we kept by the phone and wrote Lee a note.

Meet me on the front lawn first
day of school, please? — D.

I found an envelope in one of the kitchen drawers and addressed it. Even though I was still in my pajamas, I put on my flip-flops and walked out to the mailbox. The morning was warm and bright and fog-free. On the way back to the house I felt light in a way that made me want to run, so I did, which wasn't easy in flip-flops. I ran all the way back to the house, for once walking through the front door unafraid.

15 A.

And if I ever met the girl on the waves, this is what she would tell me:

Sometimes rescue comes to you.

It just shows up, and you do nothing.

Maybe you deserve it, maybe you don't.

But be ready, when it comes,

to decide if you will take the outstretched hand

and let it pull you ashore.

16.

Somehow I talked Darren into giving me a ride on the first day of school. I needed someone with me at least on the drive over because there was a good chance I'd be on my own once I got there, maybe for the whole school year.

Part of me was ready for that.

Part of me wanted to barf.

We rolled by the same old Pacifica houses we'd passed every day for years: some with cars on lawns and mildewed paint jobs, some with carefully landscaped front yards and cheerful garden gnomes. I remembered what Michael had said about why he stayed here. Not me, I thought. I'm getting out. Someday.

Darren pulled up to Terra Nova. I looked sideways, for a

second, toward my and Lee's old meeting spot on the lawn. I didn't see her. Everything in me sank. "Keep going," I said. "Don't stop."

Darren didn't move. "Deanna."

"Screw it. I'm cutting."

"You're not cutting the first day of school," he said. "I have to get to work."

"Then drop me on the corner or something, I don't care."

"She's there."

"No, she isn't."

"Yes," Darren said, "she is." He pointed and I looked again. Lee stood under the tree in the shade, setting her backpack down on the lawn. She looked up and saw us. I closed my eyes for about three seconds so that I wouldn't have to see her walk away. When I opened them, she was still there. And now Jason stood beside her.

"That's her, right?" Darren asked.

I nodded, unable to speak.

"Hey," he said.

I turned to him.

He was a man, strong and responsible and full of whatever it is that makes a person want to do the right things in life. Then he was just my brother again, and lifted his hands off the wheel like he wanted to touch me or something, only to let them fall back, saying, "You were right. We can be different from him."

I grabbed my backpack and got out, looking back at him to

show that after everything, I could still smile. He pulled away and I stood still for a minute.

Lee gave a little half wave and I started across the lawn, the longest walk of my life.

"Hey," I said when I finally got to them.

"Hi." Lee didn't exactly smile, but she didn't look like she hated me, either.

Jason mostly looked uncomfortable, hands in his pockets like usual. He caught my eye and said, "Ready for junior year?"

I let my breath out for the first time since getting out of the car and shook my head no.

Lee picked up her backpack. "Okay then," she said. "Let's go."

Acknowledgments

Mom: For teaching me to love books and stories by reading to us every night, and doing the accents.

Comrades: In my terminally flaky but obscenely talented writing group in SLC for being my best teachers, and at the Glen Workshop for reminding me I'm not alone. Special thanks to Ray Garton and Louis Greenstein for pushing me out of the nest.

The Kevin Avery section: For being there from the first word, Saturday mornings at the library, and the many years of friendship.

When things got desperate: The Utah Arts Council for prize and grant money, FPC for flexible work hours, and Lew Hancock.

The pros: My editor, Jennifer Hunt, for her warmth and wisdom, and everyone at Little, Brown who made this all so easy. Michael Bourret, for being my dream agent and understanding Deanna (and me) from the beginning.

But not least: My husband, Gordon Hultberg, for never doubting, never failing to encourage, and always being on my side.